D1374339

THE SPANISH BIT

Tug Carlyle, a fugitive on the run, helps a fourteen-year-old boy free a wolf caught in a trap. He is taken to the home the boy shares with his father, the one-time US federal marshal Walt Skinner, and so establishes a bond that will be tested to the limit. With the arrival of the posse the boy assists Tug in his escape, leaving Skinner to be hauled off to jail for helping the fugitive. How will Tug react to this?

WILL HOUSTON

◆

THE
SPANISH BIT

Complete and Unabridged

LINFORD
Leicester

First published in Great Britain in 1999 by
Robert Hale Limited
London

First Linford Edition
published 2002
by arrangement with
Robert Hale Limited
London

British Library CIP Data

Houston, Will, *1916* –
    The Spanish bit.—Large print ed.—
Linford western library
    1. Western stories
    2. Large type books
    I. Title
    813.5'4 [F]

    ISBN 0–7089–9837–2

Published by
F. A. Thorpe (Publishing)
Anstey, Leicestershire

Set by Words & Graphics Ltd.
Anstey, Leicestershire
Printed and bound in Great Britain by
T. J. International Ltd., Padstow, Cornwall

This book is printed on acid-free paper

1

Outlaw!

From a forested jumble of large rocks he could look back and see them loping over open country toward the foothills. He guessed they were about a mile away, or close to it. The rider out front was tracking, staying to one side of the shod-horse imprints.

There were four of them, each with a Winchester slung under the *rosadero* in its saddle boot.

At that distance, with the sun shifting, all he could be sure of was that they were tracking him.

They'd been closer, dangerously close back nearer the town when he'd cast free the lead rope to his pack horse to buy time. It worked, he saw them dump his panniers, free the horse and waste time sifting through his belongings. They knew his name now, but that wasn't important, widening the distance was; with luck he might have time tomorrow for reflection, right now his sole interest was in keeping far enough ahead to avoid gunfire.

Once past the foothills it was rugged country. He favoured his horse as often as he dared, but he wasn't riding a cow horse; thoroughbreds were taller and faster but not as a rule as durable and tough.

In flat country he could have lost them miles back. In this country, where rough foothills led to heavily forested uplands, no matter which way a fugitive fled, he eventually faced mountains, some enormously tall, the kind that usually retained snow caps until August, or lesser uplands as primitive as they'd always been. A thousand years of Indian habitation hadn't made a dent.

How they had happened to be waiting was a mystery. Possibly it had been only an ambush; they might have just naturally been at the livery barn, which made it possible for them to go after him almost before he cleared the north end of the town.

After so many years of perfecting what he thought was a foolproof technique, he'd ridden into a trap, or the appearance of one.

He reined up in a small vale with belly-high grass, let the tall horse sip at a creek, loosened the cinch and let him trail his reins as he ate.

It may have been a foolish thing to do, but the thoroughbred which had out-distanced his share of posses in flat country, had either to be rested, or give out. And there was the the odd feeling men formed with their saddle animals, especially single men with no families. He'd risk capture to avoid foundering his long-legged partner. If the pursuit was slowed by rugged, forested high-lands it would certainly help; the difficulty was that the animals they were riding, stock horses, were usually as tough as rawhide.

The horse returned to the piddling little coldwater creek to finish tanking up and his rider did the same.

He was flat out in the grass belly down, drinking, when a buck elk almost as tall as his saddle horse came charging out of the tree from the south. His nostrils were flared; his eyes bulged: he was running for his life.

If he saw the man and his horse at the creek he gave no indication of it when he leapt over the waterway no more than a hundred feet away and disappeared into the forest.

The man jack-knifed to his feet. Whatever had scared the daylights out of that elk was close.

It didn't seem possible. The man patted his horse, tugged it away from the creek and was leaning to cinch up when three buffalo wolves burst out of the trees from the south.

They were big animals, half again as tall as the tallest dog. Their tongues were lolling. What saved the bull elk was that he had raced past in blind terror

4

and the dog wolves delayed long enough to raise their heads; they had caught man-scent.

The thoroughbred turned and went stiff as a plank. He'd never seen buffalo wolves before but he didn't need to have; instinct told him all he had to know. The rider grabbed both reins, drew his holster Colt and waited.

The big wolves spread a little, then the dominant one turned back to the forest's protection.

The man used the tie-down thong to secure his weapon, finished cinching, turned the tall horse once and mounted.

He had covered a considerable distance when he heard it; a gunshot so distant it was barely audible. He kept on riding; now there were probably two buffalo wolves.

The gunshot had placed the pursuit. They were much further back than the fugitive thought they would be, and in consequence he no longer pushed the thoroughbred, which suited the horse fine. He was an open country animal, making haste where huge old overripe fir trees grew almost impenetrably close was not where haste was possible and the big horse was tiring.

Dusk came early in forested country. High tree-tops cut out daylight down below. The fugitive began watching for a place to hobble the horse and unroll his two old army blankets.

What he sought was an area where he could not be surprised although it was unlikely the pursuers would push ahead in darkness.

A man in the fugitive business — a *successful* man at it — took no chances he didn't have to take. The Lord knew life had a way of forcing risks on people and anyone who understood this did not otherwise run risks, although there were some professions that just naturally were riskier than others.

They continued as long as they could. It was slow going with big trees to be dodged with every other step but again, the alternative was likely to be downright unhealthy; there were trees in every direction with low limbs sticking out and those pursuers surely had lass ropes.

Once, crossing a busy snow-water creek he caught scent of smoke. He hadn't seen a person nor anything to do with them for hours.

He went wide out and around that scent which he thought might be some old coot of a trapper.

Just short of dusk, he breasted a rocky spit of land and halted on its rim. Below was a meadow, possibly a half-mile of it with tall grass, stands of thorny chaparral and three large animals grazing before sunset.

He had no idea where he was. That town back yonder was named Brighton; it was in a territory called Colorado, or maybe by now he was upcountry enough to be in Wyoming. Not that it mattered a hell of a lot, although it wasn't where he wanted to be.

New Mexico had mountains and forests, creeks and endless miles of grazing country, up north. Down south, where he had come from, forests, if they had ever existed, showed only as petrified fossil and while there was grazing, unlike the north country where one calvy cow stayed greasy fat, in lower New Mexico it required close to a couple of miles of land to support a calvy cow.

He wasn't heading in the right direction by a long shot; those hard-riding sons of bitches from that town back yonder had got between him and where he wanted to be, so with no choice he had fled northward.

Somewhere these damned mountains ended, but by failing daylight it didn't seem that way. Every side-hill he rounded showed more high country, seemingly endless miles of it.

His tall bay horse was beginning to scuff with his hind feet. He was wearing down. If there had been any flat country he couldn't have outrun a dog.

If his pursuers were still back there somewhere they'd have to stop soon.

The best sign reader on earth couldn't track in the dark, especially in country where spongy generations of fir and pine needles had been piling up for centuries.

He let the horse move out on a loose rein. It would be better able to watch its footing than the man it carried might be.

Something, probably sound, certainly not a sighting in failing daylight, spooked some animals picking brush in the burnt-off clearing. They ran for the surrounding timber and were lost to sight in moments.

There was graze and browse aplenty but no water which wouldn't bother the tucked-up thoroughbred until he got his fill of grass.

The man selected a tree, draped both his holstered sidearm and his booted Winchester from a low limb, got the circulation stirring in his legs by making a half a surround looking for water.

What he found was a piddling little spring where old tipi rings of rocks

9

showed that once there had been people up here.

It was close to the north-easterly rim of the place where he chose to bed down. He led his horse to it, the horse refused to drink so the man led him, hobbled him and unrolled his blankets.

There was no need for a fire, supper consisted of a flat tin of sardines and two lint-encrusted sticks of jerky.

It wasn't as warm a night as he was accustomed to. At the altitude he had reached there were never warm nights, not even in July and August.

He rolled in satisfied he was safe, awakened ahead of sunrise, washed and drank at the spring and stood in deafening silence watching his horse hop as it grazed along.

When the sun came it would lighten the world he had fled from but not the world where he now was; those stiff-topped big old trees would block daylight as they had been doing before Hector was a pup.

The fugitive studied his surroundings. He was lost in a timbered vastness of unimaginable size.

When he was ready to leave, he followed a line-of-sight route he'd figured out the day before. There was a dusty trail, wide enough to prevent elk antlers from snagging the low limbs of trees.

By yesterday's calculation he was satisfied that the tiers of distant peaks would stretch for many miles more. Somewhere out of the mountains there would be open country and towns, or at least settlements. It had been said that if a man rode due south long enough he would arrive where there were settlements. He knew about the south-westerly country but now he was riding north. If that old adage was true he might find a settlement within the next three or four days.

He would welcome it, his horse needed a long rest, good feed and a new set of shoes all the way around.

Those things cost money, but for one

of the few times in his life being broke or close to it was not an issue. There was enough money in his saddle-bags to carry him comfortably into old age if he didn't piss it away.

The following day he got a surprise. His study of those high old sawtooth rims which seemed to go endlessly northward gradually widened to the point when he paused to blow his animal, the peaks were still up there, stair-stepping their way one after another, but where he stopped this time there was that widening gap which got wider. He resumed the ride and those peaks continued to pull back westerly and easterly until leaving the widening gap. By the time he was in sight of the country beyond, without forested interference, he was able to see down the wide slot to open country; at least open country where the mountains pulled away.

He made a dry camp, finished the sardines and jerky, had a smoke under a tattered sky with light showing through and listened to his horse eating. There are fewer more satisfying and relaxing sounds than that made by grazing animals.

Some time in the nearly moonless night he heard a wolf wail. It wasn't the sound of foraging carnivores on the hunt and it wasn't the soulful cry of a dog wolf seeking a bitch; whatever it was it was half muted by distance so the man sank back to steal a few more hours of sleep.

The next time he awakened the leggy bay horse was lipping his face. It was filled out in the flanks, but now it was thirsty and since it served the two-legged thing it was the two-legged thing's responsibility to find it water.

They found an ancient crooked trail going down into that widening swale that got wider the further they went until with the sun over the fugitive's left shoulder it was possible to see open grassland for many miles.

Isolated or not, somewhere up ahead would be a set of buildngs. Country people, particularly livestock men, settled in such areas, built homes, corrals, barns and brought in cattle. As far as the fugitive could see there were no buildings and no cattle. For a brief period he deluded himself into thinking this might be virgin country. What spoiled that illusion was the sorrowful wail of a wolf again.

He knew that sound, wolves caught in traps made that sound. It was distinctive from their normal sounds. The Indians said it was their death-cry. Whatever it was the animal who made it was close and, because the fugitive habitually avoided open country, when he reined westerly in the direction of thickly massive encircling forest he heard it again, then the wolf was silent. It was not uncommon for them to free themselves of traps by biting off the trapped foot.

Without warning a horse nickered. It had probably detected the thorough-bred's scent.

The fugitive halted with hair on the

back of his neck standing up. There was no sound that the nickering horse had fled at his approach. There was hardly any noise at all except for a scolding blue jay high on his treetop perch.

The thoroughbred walked along with its head up, little ears pointing; it had a scent.

There were stumps; in past times someone had taken trees down, probably for buildings, in those places sunlight could penetrate.

The fugitive saw the horse first, a short-back, tiger-striped buckskin, fat as a tick with a rounded chin and good eye.

It was bridled but there was no saddle. The thoroughbred breathed a nearly indistinguishable greeting and the buckskin visibly relaxed.

Movement in forest gloom caught the man's attention. The trapped wolf hadn't been caught by the paw, it had somehow managed to get about half of its left front leg in the trap.

It was crouching, motionless and

silent. The man swung down, trailed his reins and approached. The wolf bared its teeth and snarled.

The man drew riding gloves from under his belt, pulled them on and spoke to the trapped animal.

'I'll get you out of there but if you bite me . . . ' The man moved closer, halted within six or eight feet and saw the broken foreleg.

Freeing a dog wolf with a broken leg wouldn't help a damned bit.

While he and the wolf were regarding each other, the buckskin nickered again. It and the big thoroughbred were standing statue-like looking intently north-easterly.

The man slowly turned to his left and simultaneously jerked on the tie-down thong of his holstered Colt.

2

Mary Todd

The wolf broke a tense moment with a soft groan. The intruder spoke. 'You was goin' to shoot it?'

'No, I was goin' to turn it loose until I saw the leg was broken.'

The intruder was tall, thin, dressed in patched shirt and britches and hadn't been near a pair of shearing clippers in a long time. He had no face fuzz so the fugitive guessed him to maybe shy of his teens or maybe a tad older. The youth spoke again. 'That leather on your pistol got pulled loose. My name's Jeff. What's yours?'

'Tugwell.'

The youth pondered that. 'First name or last name?'

'First name. They called me Tug since I was younger'n you.'

'Tug, you know where you are?'

'No, sir, I sure don't.'

'I didn't think so. You came up from the south?'

The man nodded and put forth a question of his own. 'You live around here, Jeff?'

'Close enough.' The shaggy head turned. 'You sure her leg's broke?'

'Pretty sure.'

'You know how to set a broke leg?'

'I can try but she's not goin' to like it.'

The thin youngster leaned an old Sharps carbine aside and walked to within a few feet of the wolf. It didn't make a sound. The boy knelt. 'It's your own fault. You know better'n to run off.'

The wolf shook just the tip of its tail. The boy turned as he fished forth a braided pigging string and said, 'I'll hold her, you spring the trap.'

The man considered the wolf. It was a young animal, a little on the gutty side. 'Is she a pet, boy?'

'You can't make a real pet of 'em, but I got her before her eyes was open so she don't wander much an' she comes back.'

'What's her name?'

'Mary Todd. My pa named her for President Lincoln's wife. She answers to just plain Mary.' The lad did what the man wouldn't have done, he reached over the wolf's head to examine the trapped leg. 'It's broke all right, mister. I'll hold her while you step on the trap an' spring it.'

The wolf cried when the trap was opened and the boy removed her leg. The fugitive wouldn't have touched that leg for a sizeable wad of greenbacks. A bitch wolf had powerful jaws and large tearing teeth. As he stepped back the man asked if the boy thought she'd follow with the broken leg and, as the lad scratched the bitch's back, he looked up.

'You boost her across my lap when I get astride.'

The man went close, sank to one

knee and stroked the wolf's head very gently. She tolerated his touch but didn't blink as she looked at him.

The man arose, 'Jeff, she's not goin' to let me pick her up. She's got a lot of pain an' I'm a stranger.'

The lad eased down the broken leg, looked over where the horses were getting acquainted by sniffing each other and stood up.

'She won't bite you. My pa says she don't know how to be mean.'

The man eyed the wolf who returned his gaze in a wary, expressionless manner. 'There's never been a wolf born that don't bite,' he said.

The boy considered the man who was not tall but muscled up like a boar bear. 'She's too heavy for me to carry. She's about two months with pups. Pet her, talk to her then we got to go.'

'We could make a sling, Jeff, and carry her.'

'There's nothing to make a sling with an' besides it'd be too far. Just let her sniff you up, talk to her. I'll get on

Buck'n you can boost her up.'

The lad impressed the man as one of those calm people who didn't get ruffled; opinionated maybe, someone who sorted things out on the spot. If he'd been either surprised or fearful at seeing the man he had given no sign of it.

The man and wolf eyed each other as the man tugged on his gloves. 'Jeff, we could knock her out.'

'She's been hurt enough. I'll get astride.'

The wolf turned long enough to watch the boy spring astraddle the short-backed buckskin then returned its gaze to the man who leaned, scratched her back, behind her ears, bent over, got both arms around her and straightened up. Except for a groan the wolf neither struggled nor growled. The man carried her over, helped the lad get her balanced and went after his thoroughbred. As they were leaving with the boy ahead he said, 'Is that there a thoroughbred horse, Tug?'

'Yes.'

'Can he run?'

'If he has to. Why?'

'Because if you come this far through the mountains an' didn't know where you was, ridin' a runnin' horse, I'd say you had a reason.'

The man did not reply.

One thing became obvious: the lad knew his territory. When they'd sashayed among huge trees awhile he abruptly changed course, came to a faint trail and followed it.

The lower open country was visible for miles. The boy didn't leave the final fringe of trees; in fact, he deliberately avoided places where the sun shone and the path he was following meandered, always angling where there was shelter.

The buckskin horse walked along as though he didn't know he instinctively should have feared wolf smell. He needed no guiding and his reins flapped loose. He knew where home was.

The man saw no buildings even after he detected the aroma of wood smoke.

Where they angled around a pointy knob with trees atop it the boy said, 'Pa'll like company. He never says anythin' but I know him; he's lonesome.'

The house came into sight at about the time the bitch wolf peed, something neither the boy nor his horse heeded although both got soaked. The lad's grip on the wolf's thick throat guardhairs was firm. As long as the wolf didn't get over-balanced on one side or the other the boy could handle her.

The man shook his head. If someone had told him they'd seen a boy riding bareback with a she wolf in his lap he wouldn't have believed them.

The cabin had been made entirely of draw-knifed logs. It had three rooms, two of which, judging by the fresher colour of the logs had been added on. There was a thin, lazy spindrift of smoke arising from a sodden sheathing which encased a metal stovepipe.

There was a corral with no horse in it, a log barn of modest size and some kind of palisaded yard with a three-sided shelter inside it.

If these things had been in a settlement or on its outskirts they wouldn't have attracted attention. As the fugitive rode closer he speculated that whoever had done the building had selected the site because it blended with its timbered surroundings, a position not to be noticed.

A man straddling a grinding wheel where he'd been putting an edge on a double bitted axe stopped pumping and sat motionless as the riders approached the yard.

As he unwound off the grinding wheel he called to the boy. 'You found her, eh?'

'In a trap Pa, with a busted leg.'

The boy's kin considered the fugitive, curtly inclined his head and said, 'Step down, mister. My name's Skinner. Walt Skinner.'

The fugitive dismounted, shook the offered calloused hand as he introduced himself. 'Tug Carlyle, Mister Skinner. I saw the wolf in the trap . . . your boy came along. We brought her home.'

'Obliged, Mr Carlyle. I been tellin' him ever since he found her they don't stay close like a dog.'

The men lifted the wolf down. She nearly fell trying to avoid putting the broken leg to the ground. Jeff's kinsman eyed her and jerked his head toward the house. 'Take her inside, boy. I'll find some sticks an' we'll splint it.'

Mary Todd followed the boy slowly, clumsily and painfully. The men watched and Tug said, 'You got a right decent spread here, Mr Skinner.'

As they eyed each other, Jeff and his bitch wolf vanished inside the log house. Skinner said, 'You come up from the south, Mr Carlyle?'

Tug nodded. 'Hard country. Where I come from they don't have so many miles of mountains.'

Walt Skinner was briefly pensive before speaking again. 'Come inside, we'll set that leg. It was decent of you to help my boy.'

The fugitive and the lad watched Walt Skinner work on the broken leg. He kept up a running conversation as he worked. 'She won't be chasin' rabbit for a spell. Jeff, you learn anythin' from this?'

'Not to set no more traps, Pa.'

'Hand me that wrap-around, please.'

Tug Carlyle moved quickly. As he handed over the bandaging he said, 'That's a real professional job, Mr Skinner,' and got back a curt reply.

'A man learns things over the years. Jeff, stoke up the stove.'

Carlyle interpreted that correctly. 'I don't want to interrupt things. I'll be on my way.'

Walt Skinner rocked back on his heels, ran a rough hand down the wolf's back as he said, 'We'd take it kindly if you'd stay. Jeff, go fire up the stove. I expect Mr Carlyle's hungry; I know I sure am.'

As the lanky youth left the parlour, Walt Skinner jack-knifed up to his feet facing the stranger from the south.

Skinner was a strong man accustomed to hard work and lots of it.

He asked a question. 'There's a town down there. Brighton.'

Carlyle nodded. 'I rode through it.'

'Did you meet folks down there, talk to them?'

Tug Carlyle had indeed met folks down there. He hadn't talked to them much but as long as he lived he would remember the town. 'Passed through is about all, Mr Skinner.'

Walt was wiping his hands on a faded old red bandanna. The wolf at his feet made a faint whimper. Skinner smiled at her. 'It'll heal, but you'll have to learn to walk three-legged, old girl.'

Skinner responded to Jeff's call from the kitchen by gesturing for Tug Carlyle to precede him.

The meal was a success, everything they ate came from inside the eight-foot-tall faggot palisade or from the hen house.

Afterwards, the men went out to sit under the wide and long overhang.

When the boy eventually came out he didn't hesitate, he said, 'I'll look after your horse, Mr Carlyle,' and hiked in the direction of the barn.

As his father watched him go, he said pensively, 'I've got to do something about schooling. I've home-taught him readin', writin' and cyphers but he needs more.' He turned his head. 'By any chance you're not a schoolteacher?'

Tug Carlyle laughed. 'For the boy's sake I wish I was.'

Walt Skinner changed the subject so abruptly it caught Tug Carlyle off guard. He said, 'A couple of years back two other strangers stopped by. They also came from the south. Bounty-huntin' manhunters. I'd guess anyone who'd buck the mountains like they did, an' like you did, with a stage road easterly only a few miles an' visible from up where you rode, would have a reason.'

Jeff called from the barn. His father shot up to his feet. The boy's call had been strident.

Both men went to the barn. The thoroughbred horse was eating cured meadow hay and ignored the trio of two-legged things.

Jeff had draped the thoroughbred's riding outfit from a saddle pole. Both men saw the unbuckled flap of Tug Carlyle's saddle-bags at the same time.

Jeff was standing close to the saddle pole.

His father said, 'Boy, you know better'n to snoop into someone else's gatherings.' He was angry and showed it.

Without a word, Jeff twisted, reached into the saddle-bag and brought forth a fistful of greenbacks.

For a long moment nothing was said, after which Walter Skinner, using the same angry tone of voice, said, 'Put 'em back! What's wrong with you, boy, searchin' someone else's outfit! Go do your chores. I'll talk to you later. *Go!*'

After Jeff had left the barn, Walt Skinner slowly faced around without saying a word until Tug Carlyle spoke.

'Now you got an answer why I come northward through those mountains.'

Walt gently nodded. 'From Brighton?'

'The bank an' mercantile down there.'

'How much?'

'I haven't counted it. A sizeable amount I expect.'

Walt blew out a ragged breath. 'You had to run for it? That means they came after you.'

Tug nodded. 'I think they gave up a few days back. At least when I watched my trail from a couple of those high peaks I didn't see anything.'

Walt went to lean on the saddle pole near the opened saddle-bag, looking steadily at Carlyle. After a while he said, 'I expected it would happen, someday, but I'll be damned if I ever thought it would be like this. Mister Carlyle, you want to talk?'

'Not much to say,' the outlaw replied. 'I didn't go there to rob the place. I been tryin' to find a brother for three years. The last notion I had took me to Brighton. It was another disappointment. No one had heard of him. 'Course he'd be using another name.'

'Why were you looking for him, Mr Carlyle?'

'He killed two men in Texas an' a year or so later he escaped from a chain gang.'

'Fair fight or murder, Mr Carlyle?'

'Murder.'

Walt straightened up off the saddle pole, reached to methodically buckle the saddle-bag flap and spoke again as he was finishing with the saddle-bag. He was silent so long Tug Carlyle looked around for something to sit on. Some hungry chickens squawking as Jeff fed them was the only noise until the outlaw said, 'I'll leave. By now my horse is ready.'

Without looking around, Walt said, 'That horse's been rode about as hard as he can go. He needs a few days . . . ' Walt turned. 'I'm goin' to tell you a story, Mr Carlyle. You maybe noticed how our place here is hid from sight.'

Tug nodded, he had indeed noticed — and wondered.

'You know anythin' about the Minnesota raid by the James boys and their kinsmen?'

Again Tug nodded, that attempted robbery and subsequent shootout that had left dead outlaws propped against the front of a store, hadn't happened long enough before not to still be a source of newspaper headlines and frenzied front-page reporting.

Walt made a wry small sardonic smile.

'You was there, Mr Skinner?'

'I was there. Folks knew they were coming. It was like butchering hogs, even storekeepers were waiting, everybody an' his brother was armed. It sounded like war.'

Walt returned to leaning on the saddle pole as Tug asked another question. 'How'd you escape?'

This time Walt Skinner answered

without hesitation. 'I was the telegrapher. Worked for the railroad until I quit an' joined the federal marshals.'

There was no need for Tug Carlyle to ask the obvious question. Newspaper accounts said a federal marshal was the one who got things organized.

'You?'

'Yes.'

Tug went to lean on the log wall near the front opening. 'Why'd you quit up there?'

Walt made a death's-head smile. 'I'm the one who's supposed to be asking the questions.' He gave Tug Carlyle no opportunity to answer. 'I quit for the same reason we come out this far an' made our hideaway. It only took a few weeks to turn the federal marshal up there from a hero to a bushwhackin' son of a bitch. Jesse an' his family was folk heroes. I got faced down a few times an' I got threats. They said I was a coward; that I set up the Jameses, that it was pure murder an' I was responsible. I had Jeff to think about. His ma died at childbirth. You can guess the rest of it.'

'Folks around here don't know?' Tug asked. 'Isn't there a town, neighbours?'

Again Skinner made that death's-head small smile. 'The name of that federal marshal was Spencer. Ray Spencer. Even blind folks could read that name. Folks got to comparin' Ray Spencer with Benedict Arnold. Mister Carlyle, you know what's ironic about this? If I throw down on you an' take you down to Brighton for the law, sure as I'm standin' here someone'll make the connection between Walt Skinner an' Ray Spencer.' The humourless smile lingered. 'A pair of renegades, an outlaw an' a lawman . . . They got the time to hunt you down.'

'I'll be long gone, Mr Skinner.'

The remark earned a head-shake of disagreement. 'It won't matter. They'll track you to our place, ask questions about me'n Jeff, about why we're back here out of sight. I know something about manhunting, Mr Carlyle; when you can't get your man you invent him, find someone who's living in a secret place who sheltered a fugitive riding a long-legged thoroughbred horse an' before you know it I'm either the outlaw or a friend, maybe an accomplice of his. One thing lawmen can't abide; end up lookin' bad.'

Tug straightened up off the wall. 'Tell 'em whatever you want. Let 'em do their trackin'. By the time they get this far I'll be so far off . . . '

'Not on that horse, Mr Carlyle.'

Tug leaned against the logs again. That was the truth, his handsome big breedy animal hadn't been bred for this kind of country.

Jeff appeared in the doorway. He looked from his father to Tug and back. 'She's tryin' to walk, Pa.'

The three of them went to the house and sure enough the wolf was standing on three feet trying to put weight on the fourth leg.

3

A Constable

For Tug Carlyle the only recourse appeared to be to get on his way without delay. Another time he might have laughed at a situation where a lawman and an outlaw had by some ironic twist of fate been brought together in the face of the serious enmity of others.

Tug went to watch his thoroughbred graze. As far as the horse was concerned Tug could have been on Mars.

There was an additional difficulty: the big horse had cast one shoe somewhere and the remaining three were worn down past gnarled nail heads.

He was joined out in the pasture by Walt Skinner who said, 'Mister Carlyle, since we're likely to be stuck to one another for a spell we could use first names. I'm Walt.'

Carlyle looked around. 'Tug. Name's Tugwell but I've always been called Tug.'

Skinner accepted that and asked a question. 'Did anyone get hurt down in Brighton?'

'Not as far as I know; only my professional pride as an outlaw. With all the shooting they did an' I didn't get hit; my shootin' back until my gun was spent was done on a horse runnin' for all he was worth.' Tug paused. 'Someday I'd like to find out how they come onto me so quick.'

Skinner mentioned another subject. 'Upcountry a ways at Bridgeport, they got a telegraph.'

Tug stared. He didn't recall seeing a telegraph office in Brighton, but if there had been one and they sent word south to the next town to watch for a stranger riding a big bay thoroughbred . . .

He said, 'Son of a bitch,' and Walt

nodded understandably. 'Trapped in front an' in back.'

Tug considered the dark and rugged uplands. He wasn't sure where he was and if he took to more mountains to elude pursuers, it wouldn't matter where he was as long as he kept ahead.

He looked at his grazing horse. Walt did the same and noticed one barefoot and three shod ones worn down to the quick. Walt said nothing but it was beginning to dawn on him, whether he liked it or not — and he didn't like it — he and the outlaw had been cast by a perverse fate into the same boat.

It was dusk when they returned to the house. Jeff was bedded down; where there was no electricity and coal oil for lamps was costly, folks bedded down early. It was candles and bed down early.

The following day Walt rassled breakfast. When Tug asked about the boy he got a short reply.

'Gone back south a ways to see if

they're still on your trail.'

Tug was raising the coffee cup when he said, 'An' if they are?'

'Why then I'd say the telegrapher at Brighton's contacted his friend up at Bridgeport.'

Tug changed the subject. 'Do you happen to have a forge an' maybe some spare horseshoes?'

'I cold shoe our saddle animal, the buckskin. He's got feet big as a dinner plate. I got no forge to make 'em small enough for your bay.'

Tug looked steadily at his host. 'Are you gettin' a feelin' that for some damned reason we're being bottled up in a situation that don't have no answers, no way out?'

'I got that feelin' last night. You mind answerin' a question?'

Tug was too worried to mind. He said, 'Shoot.'

'Have you always been an outlaw?'

'Not always, only after I was big enough to hold a gun an' ride a fast horse.'

'It don't pay, Tug. I've run down a few an' they all said it don't pay.'

Tug's steely grey-blue eyes faintly twinkled. 'What else would they say? It'll pay, Walt, sometimes not real well, other times like down at Brighton it pays good.'

'Risky business, Tug.'

'So's gettin' on a strange horse or meetin' up with painted tomahawks. Life's a risk, Walt. Take marriage . . . '

From a distance someone made a powerful two-fingered whistle. Walt said, 'He's back.'

They went back to the log barn where Jeff was off-saddling a sweaty buckskin horse. As he grunted the saddle up onto its pole he said, 'There's riders comin' south, likely from Bridgeport.' When his father asked how many the boy held up four fingers and a thumb. 'There was sunlight bouncin' off booted guns.'

'On the road?' his father asked.

'Skirtin' along the edge of the timberland.'

Tug had a question. 'No sign from the south?'

'No, but there could be. There's too many trees.'

Except for the booted saddle guns neither of the men would have worried. As Jeff returned from caring for the buckskin he said, 'If they're comin' here, it'll be a while. They was about two miles off.'

The federal marshal faced Tug Carlyle with an unspoken question and the fugitive jerked his head. After the two men were in the yard Tug said, 'I'd better be on my way,' and got a short answer.

'On a wore-down horse leavin' sign you been here?'

'You got a better idea?'

'It might not be better but we don't have a lot of time. If you want 'em off your trail give me your saddle-bags. I'll give them to 'em. They might be willin' to settle for that. If they will why then you can be on your way. Go west. About a day's ride there's a

41

settlement called Meadows. Home-steader country.'

Tug was momentarily silent, the money in his saddle-bags was what he'd figured to use buying a one-man cow outfit where he'd settle down.

Walt misjudged the silence. He sounded slightly irritable when he spoke again. 'They'll find you. I know, I did my share of manhuntin'. If you're here when they arrive they'll most likely take me back with you for harbourin' a criminal.'

Jeff crossed from the barn in the direction of the house. He was not only hungry, he was worried about Mary Todd. The men were silent until the door slammed then Tug said, 'I figured to use that money to get set up somewhere.'

This time his host's irritability was obvious. 'They'll never let up. If they don't catch you here they'll catch you somewhere. How much money you got?'

Tug hadn't counted it. He probably

could have but his overriding anxiety had been escape. 'I don't know.'

'You didn't count it?'

'No. I was too busy stayin' ahead.'

Skinner let his shoulders sag and wagged his head. 'You can't be here when they arrive. I got Jeff. If they send me away . . . we're wastin' time. If I had a better horse I'd trade you.'

Tug interrupted. 'If you had my thoroughbred they'd know. By now those fellers from Brighton know what I was ridin' was better'n anything they had.'

Skinner turned impatiently toward the barn for a catch rope to use bringing in the thoroughbred. As Tug moved to follow, Jeff gave a warning whistle from the house.

Both men ducked inside the barn. Walt swore under his breath. He didn't wear a sidearm around his home place.

There was a small loft under the peaked roof, not high enough for a man to stand up in. It was better than half full of fragrant meadow hay. Walt jerked his head. 'Get up there.'

As Tug climbed the loft pole he wasn't satisfied hiding in the loft would do more than cause a delay. His thoroughbred horse was visible from the rear barn opening.

Jeff called mutedly from the porch. 'In the trees, comin' uphill from the north-east. Just a glimpse of 'em.'

His father took a three-tined hay fork from its nails and walked over the palisaded vegetable patch. He was sifting mulch when four riders rode clear of timber coming in the direction of his yard.

He went back, leaned the fork aside, mopped off sweat and waited. There should have been five unless Jeff had miscounted.

He hadn't, there were five, one rider was circling back through the trees to come in from the north-west. As surely as God had made green apples he was going to see the thoroughbred.

The foremost horseman was an unshaven, thickly built, greying man whose badge hadn't been polished in a 'coon's age. His name was Ames Felton. He was a town constable. His authority normally extended to the town limits of Bridgeport but in a country of vast distances and questionable county lines, constables served where a county sheriff should have. There was another factor: constables were paid a lot less than genuine sheriffs.

The men with Ames Felton were a mixed crew; two were obviously rangemen, the other one was just as clearly a townsman. They looked capable and while Constable Felton spoke to Walt Skinner his riders studied the house, the barn, outbuildings and the corral with its sweat-drying buckskin horse.

Ames Felton and Walt Skinner were acquaintances rather than friends. Folks in his town knew Skinner as a reclusive individual, something not unusual in their country. The storekeeper said Skinner ran a bill and paid promptly. For him that was all he had to know to approve of an individual.

Ames Felton stood with his horse, trailing both reins as he too looked around and addressed Skinner.

'There's a feller robbed the store an' bank down at Brighton an' run for it northward. They telegraphed us. Walt, he's got to be somewhere between down there an' up here. He didn't use the coach road.'

That fifth posse rider walked his horse into the yard, leaned on his saddle horn and ignored Walt to address the constable.

'There's a thoroughbred horse hobbled out a ways from the barn, Ames.'

The lawman raised a hand to tip his hat as he looked steadily at Walt, whose insides balled up before the constable said, 'Walt . . . where is the son of a bitch?'

The answer came from an open loft door at the barn. It was followed by the sound of a weapon being cocked.

'Get down. All of you. Keep both

hands where I can see 'em! Good; now shuck the guns. Carbines too . . . you gents're real co-operative.'

One of the rangemen replied sourly, 'Right now it pays to be.'

Ames Felton was a blustery individual. He shed his guns but retained the reins and faced the barn. 'There's a bounty on you. You can't stay in that loft forever. All we got to do is set down an' wait you out.'

Ames shifted his attention to Walt Skinner. 'How long you been hidin' the son of a bitch, Walt? He pay you, did he?'

Skinner reddened. 'One day, Ames, an' I'll let that pass about payin' me.'

'You knew who he was; a gawd-damned bank-robbin' outlaw an' you a federal lawman?'

Tug Carlyle spoke before Walt could. 'Take the bridles'n saddles off those horses an' turn 'em loose.'

An unhappy rangeman squinted in the barn's direction. 'You got any idea how long a walk it will be gettin' back?'

47

'Never been to your place, mister. *Off-rig them horses!*'

Ames Felton was the only intruder who made no move to obey. As the others were sullenly removing saddles, blankets and bridles, Felton said, 'Mister, they're on their way from the south. Even on foot we can block you from goin' anywhere. You want some advice? Hand over what you stole an' I'll lock you up in Bridgeport so's those fellers from Brighton can't hang you.'

Jeff coming from the house provided a temporary diversion.

The constable said, 'What's he up to, Walt?'

'Goin' to feed the chickens.'

'Is he armed?'

Walt's sound of disgust was unmistakable when he replied, 'He's only a fourteen-year-old kid, for Chris'sake.'

Ames replied without taking his eyes off the boy. 'So was Jesse James when he went bad.' Felton raised his voice. 'Stay were I can see you, boy. Walt?'

'What?'

48

'You better talk your friend down out of there. The way it looks right now, you're aidin' an outlaw.'

Skinner brusquely looked in the direction of the loft door. He saw nothing; the loft door was small; it was also the only way for daylight to get into the loft. He faced the constable. 'He come here on a tired horse, hungry'n wore down. That's no crime.'

'But harbourin' an outlaw is. Now tell me you didn't know he was an outlaw?'

That unhappy rangeman spoke from several feet behind the constable. 'I could use a drink of water'n so could my horse.'

Tug Carlyle spoke from the loft. 'The trough's in plain sight. Help yourself.'

The rangeman, a lean, weathered and unshaven individual said, 'So's you can shoot me in the back?'

The answer was sharp. 'Shootin' folks in the back more'n likely is what possum-belly there would do. Me, I don't. Go get your water.'

For as long as was required, attention was on the rangeman who led his animal to the trough, draped his hat, splashed water in his face and also drank.

When he finished, he looked in the direction of the loft door and said, 'Much obliged.'

There was no response.

Ames Felton raised his voice. 'Mister, you keep on doin' what you're at right now an' you're goin' to get killed. Those riders from Brighton won't be in a good mood.'

There was no response. One of the other possemen, possibly emboldened by the rangeman, also addressed the barn loft.

'Mister, it don't make no difference to me how long you stay up there but Ames wasn't lyin'. There's riders comin' from Brighton. You can give up to us or set up there an' get yourself killed.'

Aside from being the longest diatribe so far from the possemen, there was, once again, no response.

The townsmen were impatient, they had things to do back in Bridgeport. Unlike the rangemen, they had schedules. One of them, a portly, short individual with elegant sleeve garters addressed the constable. 'You said it'd take maybe two, three hours.'

That annoyed the local lawman. 'How'n hell could I know he'd be hidin' up here!' Felton raised his voice. 'You hungry yet, up there, or maybe thirsty? Like I already told you, we can set down an' worry you out, 'n if you wait, sure as hell those boys from Brighton'll hang you from a tree.'

Walt Skinner turned his head slowly. There hadn't been a sound from the loft for a long while. His faint frown activated that rangeman who had watered at the trough. He tipped his hat forward regarding the loft. Eventually he said, 'Ames, I'll bet you a new hat he ain't up there.'

That remark galvanized them all. During their anxious silence Jeff came from the direction of the chicken house. Without looking in his father's direction or the direction of the possemen he crossed to the house, entered and slammed the door after himself.

That weathered, wiry rangeman said, 'Son of a bitch!'

At the same time they all heard it, a running horse.

Constable Felton was slow getting astride. His companions were hurriedly resaddling, got astride and were crossing the yard in the direction of the running horse when Felton looked venomously at Walt and said, 'You're goin' to hang right beside him . . . you a federal lawman!'

Walt watched them leave the yard in a flinging rush. When they were gone, he turned toward the house. Jeff was standing over there. His father said, 'Boy, you've really got us into trouble this time,' and Jeff hiked toward the house.

Jeff's explanation was simple; he owed the fugitive for helping save the life of Mary Todd who was beginning to like being allowed indoors and being fussed over.

She had developed a knack of getting up and lying down with the stiffly bandaged leg. It was in her favour that she was a bitch wolf. A dog wolf would have spent as long as it took to chew off the bandage.

The boy was kneeling beside his wolf when his father came inside. He barely more than looked up as his father ranted.

When Walt was finished, he stood a moment looking down before going to the kitchen to grope along a high shelf for a partially depleted bottle of Jack Daniels and hoisting the bottle to swallow twice before replacing it.

Jeff looked at his father who returned to the parlour. 'I climbed over the fence, snuck inside, got up to the loft and told him I'd fetch the horse from out back.' Jeff made no effort to hide his pride at succeeding to help Tug Carlyle escape.

His father dropped down on a chair. There was no doubt in his mind what Ames Felton would do next: he would arrest them both.

Later, Walt might appreciate the situation of a lawman helping an outlaw but at the moment what worried him more than being hauled up to the Bridgeport jailhouse, was his son.

Judges west of the Missouri River were traditionally hard on law-breakers. In his case, a federal lawman, it required no great amount of pensiveness to know what his personal fate would be. And that meant his son would be not only motherless but also fatherless.

He went after another couple of swallows from the Jack Daniels. Later, while Jeff was feeding Mary Todd, someone yelled from the yard.

The day was ending. Walt left the house with solid misgivings. That weathered, unsmiling, leathery rangeman was sitting atop a tired horse beside Ames Felton. The cowboy did not nod as was customary when Walt came from the house.

Constable Felton leaned with both forearms atop his saddle horn. He had to switch a cud of molasses cured from one cheek to the other before he said, 'We got his horse. It's limpin' bad in front. It cast a shoe somewhere and went tender footed a coupla miles toward that squatter settlement. The boys is leadin' it back but it can't walk very good. Walt; you're under arrest. I expect you know that. Saddle up your buckskin an' ride along with me to town.'

'Ames, I can't leave the boy.'

'Sure you can. He's plenty big an' savvy to take care of himself.' The constable swung his head toward the rangeman. 'Sam, go with him. If he looks like he's goin' to run off, shoot him.'

As the rangeman dismounted to obey, he dryly said, 'Never been a buckskin born that could outrun a chicken. Let's go, mister.'

As the prisoner and the rangeman went to the barn, the constable dismounted, led his horse to the trough, waited until it had filled up then blew out a ragged sigh and went to work building a smoke.

Dusk was settling. By the time he got back to Bridgeport the café would be locked up for the night. Someone had once told Ames Felton there were serious consequences to being unmarried. Before he got to town with his prisoners he would willingly agree with that; in this life there were blessed few unmarried men who didn't occasionally go hungry and tonight he would be one of them.

4

Getting a Horse

Jeff watched the trio leave the yard, his father between the other two, riding their only horse. He fired up the mud-stoned wattle fireplace, made sure Mary Todd was close to the hearth, got the lantern lighted in the kitchen and ate a half-hearted supper.

It was full dark when he heard someone bitterly complaining about leading a three-legged horse. He didn't see them but heard them pass eastward beyond the nearest fringe of trees.

He wasn't sleepy so he sat in fireplace warmth with his bitch wolf. When she whined he got her a pan of water. It began to dawn on him that Mary Todd was developing a domesticated attitude about being cared for.

If there was a moon he didn't know;

nights in high country can be darker than the inside of a boot. Mary Todd abruptly raised her head, listening. Jeff went after his father's six-gun, went near the door, listening, and when he heard the faint but unmistakable sound of spurs, he cocked the gun, cracked the door a few inches and waited. If those townsmen thought they could catch him sleeping they were in for one hell of a surprise. He had never shot a man in his life, but as that faintly musical sound got closer to the house he raised the gun. For most things there had to be a first time.

By peeking he could make out the silhouette. He let the man get close then opened the door, raised the gun and cocked it. That sound stopped the dark shadow in its tracks. It spoke softly.

'Walt? It's me, Tug Carlyle.'

Jeff opened the door without lowering the gun. 'They come back for Pa some time back. I heard 'em say your horse give out on you.'

Tug came closer as Jeff eased off the hammer and lowered the gun. He said, 'I'm hungrier'n a bitch wolf, boy.'

Jeff stepped aside. 'They went past leadin' your lamed-up horse. There's stew in the kitchen.' Jeff led the way. Mary Todd brushed the hearth several times with her tail, something neither the boy nor the outlaw noticed.

As Tug sat down and leaned back for Jeff to put a full plate in front of him he said, 'You got any neighbours where a man could borrow a horse?'

There were no neighbours. Jeff shook his head as he pushed a thick crockery mug of black coffee in front of Carlyle. 'Not for more miles than a man could walk before sun-up.'

Tug paused to smile. 'I owe you for gettin' me out of that mess.'

Jeff ignored that. 'They'll lock Pa up in the Bridgeport jailhouse.'

Tug finished stuffing himself, pushed back and built a brown-paper smoke. 'I'll take care of that tomorrow. Right now I'd like to crawl back into the loft an' sleep.'

'Take care of it — how?'

As Carlyle arose he said, 'Trade with 'em. Me for your pa. See you in the mornin', an' again, I got to say I sure owe you, boy.'

As they entered the parlour Mary Todd made a soft little sound and Tug altered course from the door, dropped to one knee and examined the bandaged leg. She'd gnawed it but not enough for it to be rebandaged. As Tug scratched her back she licked his hand twice. As he was arising Mary Todd made a low growl. Both men looked down. She hadn't made that sound at them, she was looking in the direction of the door.

Tug grabbed the boy's arm. Jeff understood and led the way to a niche of a storeroom with shelves of 'put up' food. He dropped to his knees, pulled at a panel and when it opened he said, 'Be cramped. Get in, I'll close the openin'.'

Cramped was an understatement. Tug had his knees under his chin as the boy fastened the door from outside.

The boy returned to the parlour to sit with his wolf. She was still poised from either a sound or a scent. The last time she growled someone threw a rock against the door.

Jeff was straightening up when a man called, 'Whoever's in there come out with your hands atop your head.' When Jeff did not appear the same rough voice called again, 'You got a minute, mister, then we'll set fire an' burn you out.'

There was no question about the caller's sincerity. Jeff went to the door, opened it and stepped out. There were two of them, darkness made them unrecognizable at the moment, but when one moved, the sound of spurs inclined the boy to suspect he was the other rangeman who'd been with the constable.

The man was holding a six-gun at his side. 'All of you. Your pa an' that

61

other son of a bitch.'

'The constable an' a rangeman came by hours ago an' took my pa away with 'em.' It sounded like the truth because it was the truth. The second man spoke to his companion. 'He's lyin', Eb.'

Eb hesitated. 'You got a gun, boy?'

'Yes. My pa's Colt.'

'I mean you got it in your hand?'

'No.'

'You better not be storyin' to us, boy. We're comin' inside.'

Jeff stepped clear of the doorway. As the last man entered, he closed the door and turned. 'Leave the door open, boy.'

Jeff reopened it. The first man was already in the kitchen. They too were hungry. Jeff stood in the doorway watching them fill plates with stew. They ate standing up. Both men had the tie-down thongs hanging loose for swift access to their belt-guns.

Between mouthfuls, one of them asked Jeff where his pa kept his cache. Jeff lied for the first time. 'We don't have a cache. Pa keeps the money in his pocket purse. Go ahead an' look.' They finished wolfing down food. As one of them put his empty plate aside he said, 'We got that outlaw's crippled-up damned horse outside . . . he'll need your buckskin. We'll set an' wait for him.'

Jeff said, 'The buckskin's the only horse we got. Pa rode it when he went with the constable.'

'Any other horses close by?'

'Not for six, eight miles, over in the direction of the other homesteader place.'

That seemed to silence the possemen for a while. One drank a cupful of tepid coffee while his companion went through the house. Mary Todd growled and the man considered her. 'Got a busted leg?' he asked.

'Got it caught in a trap.'

'Is she a full-blood wolf?'

'Yes. I found her when she was a pup.'

'I got no use for wolves, crippled or any other.' As the man said that he drew his six-gun.

Jeff stepped in front of his wolf.

The second man came from the kitchen. He'd found the bottle of Jack Daniels which he held up for his partner to see. The man with the gun leathered it and took the bottle. They both drank but on a full stomach the whiskey would have a delayed reaction.

They went through the house. One of them found a tiny box with a gold ring in it which he pocketed and tossed its box aside. They looked in the cramped little storeroom and one made an admiring comment. 'You'n your pa must be pretty handy. You got enough food in here to last a real bad winter.'

When they returned to the parlour, one of them took down Walter Skinner's carbine from its antler rack above a faded tintype picture of a young woman. He ignored the picture to work the lever and satisfy himself the Winchester was loaded.

He jerked his head and got as far as the door when his partner said, 'Boy, do you smoke?'

Jeff shook his head.

'Eb, you smell it? Someone's been smokin' in here.'

His partner wrinkled his nose before speaking. 'It's real faint . . . Boy, does your pa smoke?'

Jeff told his second lie. 'Yes.'

As they went out into the yard, the posseman with the carbine said, 'Boy, don't do anythin' foolish. We'll burn you inside the house.'

Jeff watched them get astride, pick up the slack on the lame thorough-bred and fade in the south-easterly darkness.

When Tug was able to extricate himself from the tiny storage closet he had a question. 'What do you use that for?'

'Keepin' onions an' garlic cool an' out of the light.'

'Are they gone?'

'Yes. They took my ma's weddin'

65

ring. It's gold an' my pa isn't goin' to like that.'

'Do you know either of 'em?'

'No, but one called the other one Eb. I think maybe I've seen him in Bridgeport but that's a guess . . . Your big horse is limpin' real bad. At the rate they're goin' they won't reach the settlement until daylight an' it's only a few miles.'

Tug built and lighted a smoke. Jeff wrinkled his nose. 'They smelt cigarette smoke. I told 'em Pa smoked. He don't but that's all I could think of.'

Tug jackknifed his legs a few times to get the kinks out, sat down gingerly and said, 'I'm goin' after 'em.'

'In the dark on foot?'

'Boy, I got to have a horse.'

'What about Pa?'

As Tug was arising he dryly said, 'Yeah . . . boy, does your pa own a belly-gun?'

'He gave my mother one years back. You want it?' Without awaiting an answer Jeff disappeared in a bedroom and returned shortly carrying a nickel-plated under-and-over derringer of large calibre.

As Tug took it, he asked about bullets. There was none. His mother had never fired the weapon. She did not like even having guns in the house.

Tug considered the boy. He'd had to grow up fast and he'd done a good job of it. Tug gripped his shoulder. 'Your pa'll be along, boy. Take care of Mary Todd. Which way did they go?'

Jeff pointed, followed Carlyle to the door and shortly lost sight of him.

The night was wearing along. There wasn't much to be told from the position of the moon but it was chilly which signified the night was well advanced.

Tug had left his spurs back at the cabin; they only marginally hindered walking but on a clear, chilly night the faintest sound carried, and he was no more accustomed to walking than were most men who went a-horseback, but with reason to hasten he did the best he could considering the darkness, the trees and that the men he wanted were not only up ahead but were also a-horseback.

He consoled himself; it could have been daylight and hot.

Stopping often to listen eventually offered a reward but not until he had bumped into a tree, nearly fallen a dozen times and had muscle cramps from making haste.

What kept him going beyond the point where he was tempted to sit somewhere and consider other ways to help the man and boy who had done so much to help him, was a horse stumbling among rocks.

It was close. If there had been any distance involved, he would have been unable to pick up the sound.

He had made better time than he thought, otherwise there were two possibilities, either the men he wanted had stopped for some reason, or the sound had been made by a stray animal.

He slackened his pace, avoided making noise and with very limited visibility sensed rather than groped his way.

The second time he heard a steel shoe strike something solid the noise came from a different direction, more northerly.

He held the stubby litle belly-gun. If it had been loaded its range was limited. Tug knew from experience belly-guns were the most undependable weapons on earth. Somewhere up ahead were his saddle-bags stuffed with money. Right at this moment he would have traded straight across for a loaded Colt. He had cussed after he found his was missing when he had had to leave the lame thoroughbred.

A low flying owl adroitly weaved among the trees and came so close Tug could hear its wings. Part of an owl's protection was soundless flight.

Tug thrust up both hands. The owl performed a spectacular manoeuvre and disappeared.

Sounds carried but no great distance in forests. Tug was sweating inside his coat despite the chill. He paused to raise a sleeve to his face when a man with a gravelly voice said, 'What're you goin' to do with your share?'

The answer was so delayed in coming it appeared there might be no reply.

'Get the hell out of this country, find me a woman, some whiskey and . . . what the hell money you talkin' about? Ames didn't say what the bounty would be.'

Gravel-throat's answer was laconically given. 'I was thinkin' of the other money; them saddle-bags Ames took with him.'

This time the silence was more prolonged but eventually was broken. 'You mean . . . hold up the constable?'

'No other way we're goin' to get it.'

'Jack . . . ?'

'How much money was in them bags?'

'I don't know but they was full, a man could tell that from the way they was pooched out.'

'You ever do this before?'

'Once, when I was learnin' to shave. It was an old peddler. Got sixteen dollars. You?'

'No, never.'

'You got the guts?'

'I got 'em. I'm dog-ass tired of twelve dollars a month an' beans.'

Tug inched ahead. They were sitting on headhung horses rolling cigarettes. When the first match flared Tug clearly saw the face. The second match flared inside a hat. This time the face was blurry.

They were both strangers; at least, Tug didn't recognize either of them.

He moved toward them with the little lady's gun up and ready. 'Don't even breathe!'

The horseman putting his hat on had his right hand in the air. His companion froze.

'Shuck the guns. Either of you so much as wink . . . *shuck 'em!*'

Two discarded six-guns made a

muted sound as they struck spongy needles.

'Now get down! On the right side facin' me!'

One horse jerked its head. The other horse appeared not to mind his rider was dismounting on the wrong side.

Tug picked up one of the six-guns, pocketed the derringer and pointed to a coiled lariat. 'Take it down,' he told the tallest man. 'You there, back up to that tree with your hands in back.'

The tallest man went to the tree. Tug told his companion to tie his wrists behind around the tree and cocked the six-gun.

'Tight, or I'll blow your damned head off.'

As the tall man was being tied he said, 'Hell, I know who you are. I thought Ames'n the others got the buckskin horse.'

Tug ignored the speaker, aimed the six-gun at the second man and said, 'Shed your boots. Don't stand there with your mouth open. Shed 'em!'

The man dropped the tag end of the lariat and kicked out of his boots. As he did this he said, 'Mister, you want your saddle pockets back?'

Tug sneered, told the speaker to get belly down and lashed his arms in back with the man's own belt. He pulled so hard the face-arms down man groaned through clenched teeth.

The tall man watched Tug leather the six-gun that belonged to him and said, 'Jack'n me'll help you get them saddle-bags.'

Tug picked the youngest horse, snugged up and swung aboard. As he was settling the reins he said, 'Sure you would. I'm right grateful for the offer. I got a better idea,' he drew the six-gun, aimed and cocked it. 'Blow your head off.'

The tall man, unable to move, nevertheless squirmed. As Tug put up the gun and kneed the horse the tall man spoke to his companion. 'I'd settle for just the damned bounty on him. I give eighteen dollars for that Colt

. . . Can you get loose?'

The reply came petulantly. 'My arms is tingling . . . which way'd he go?'

'Toward Bridgeport.'

'We got to get loose. I'd've thrown down on him but he plumb surprised me. Can you get slack in that rope?'

The tall man squirmed and struggled. His reward was about six or eight inches of slack. He said, 'Get up on to your knees, hop around behind an' untie that knot with your teeth.'

'Can't do that, Eb. They'll come out.'

'What?'

'I got store-bought teeth. They'll come out if I latch on to that rope an' pull.'

'Well, for Chris'sake. I never knew you had store-bought teeth.'

'Most folk can't tell. They fit well enough but they'd come out if I pulled on that rope.'

The tall man strained and twisted until he had another few inches of slack. As he was doing this he spoke between grunts. 'I want my Colt back an' along with it I want that son of a bitch's scalp.'

'Eb?'

'What!'

'How'd he get from back yonder to where he come on to us?'

'With wings! Stand up'n turn your back so's you can feel the rope.'

It worked but both men were sore and sweating by the time the tall one shook off the rope and bent to free his companion.

As the freed man was threading the belt back through its trouser loops he said, 'You know how far it is?'

'Don't start complainin', just walk. If we can't get them saddle-bags from the constable maybe we can find that son of a bitch an' steal 'em back from him.'

Predawn was breaking and some-where in the north-westerly distance a staggy buck elk bellowed for a mate.

5

Bridgeport

The young horse took long steps, desirable in a saddle animal. It also jerked the reins for slack and grabbed grass stalks as it went along which was not desirable in a saddle animal, but Tug didn't take up slack, the horse was a good walker. By the time a man gets a few strands of grey around the ears he learns that everything in life is a trade-off. He had taken the best of the two horses and run off the other one.

The horse seemed to have the homing instinct most horses lacked, Tug didn't have to touch his neck with the reins to avoid trees. By the time he could look down, despite of poor light he thought he could see a coach road. An hour later he was sure of it. A morning stage rattled past south bound.

It rode high on its springs which was recognizable from the way it swayed and bounced. It had no freight although it might have a passenger or two.

Tug paralleled the road without sacrificing his timber shelter, but eventually he reached stumpover side-hills where a number of trees had been felled for houses, barns and fences.

He could have angled uphill back to the trees but didn't. This close to the village it wouldn't be uncommon for there to be visible horsemen.

Where an overgrown logging skid road went downslope he stopped. Bridgeport was about half the size of that town back yonder called Brighton. Because it was early — and chilly — there was cook-stove smoke arising and the occasional racket of horses, mules and milk cows, complaining vocally.

Bridgeport straddled a north-south wide roadway. On the east side there was a scattering of connecting pole corrals, obviously where driven cattle were held during a drive to railhead.

Tug eased the horse downslope. Where he met the coach road and his mount would have turned north from habit, Tug growled and made it cross over and walk into timber.

It was impossible to discern which building was the lawman's. There was a sign for a harness works, a store and a café. The latter sign interested him most, for the time being anyway.

He left the horse tied to a high limb, resettled his britches and both belts and started walking. Bridgeport was stirring but not greatly. It was only shortly after daybreak.

The eatery had one window facing the road and it was steamed up but the roadway door was locked. He rapped twice before the proprietor appeared, wiping his hands on a flour-sack apron, unlocked and opened the door and without a word went back to the kitchen.

Tug sat on a stool, leaned on the counter and waited. He was in only a moderate hurry. When the proprietor appeared, Tug got a shock. Her name was Beth Holden. He had known her six years earlier down along the border. She was as surprised as he was. She smiled, 'Tug!'

He grinned, 'I had no idea you'd be up here in Colorado.'

She gave gave him a penetrating look. 'This is Wyoming, Tug . . . You look hungry.' As she was turning away she also said, 'You need a shave.'

By the time the meal arrived, the woman had three more patrons, townsmen from the looks of them. They exchanged the customary nod with Tug, gave their orders and waited as Tug had done.

One of them was likely a storekeeper; he had elegant embroidered sleeve garters holding his sleeves in place.

The other two were nondescript, but, as the café warmed up, Tug picked up an unpleasant scent. It seemed to come from the short, massively muscled one of the three diners. Tug pegged him immediately; he was a blacksmith. Sooner or later they all acquired that smell; it came from handling the hooves of horses with the thrush, and soap and water barely made a dent in the aroma.

The woman flashed a smile as she slid Tug's breakfast in front of him, went further along and carefully put three other platters in front of her other customers. She'd balanced those three plates on one arm. Beth Holden had owned eateries for ten years. She was crowding forty and looked twenty.

Tug dawdled. The three villagers, with work to tend to, ate and departed. Beth leaned on the counter. Her smile would melt the *cojones* off a brass monkey.

'It's been years, Tug.'

He nodded. 'Six, eight? How'd you come to end up here in Bridgeport?'

'My husband came from here . . . he died three years back. I opened the café.' She gazed toward the wide roadway. 'It's peaceful, pretty and off by itself.' She abruptly changed the subject as she looked straight at him. 'I heard a couple of years back you'd . . . '

He looked steadily back.

'Robbed a mercantile down in Deming.'

He held up his cup. As she moved to refill it, he said, 'You can hear anythin' if you live long enough,' and they both laughed. 'Beth, where's the constable's office?'

She raised an arm. 'Over yonder on the far side of the road three doors.' She lowered the arm. 'You know him?'

'Sort of. You know him?'

'As well as I want to. Since my husband died he's been comin' here almost every day.' She leaned closer. 'He's a tub of lard.' She paused. 'I'm just talkin'. It wouldn't be worth repeating.'

Tug arose to fish for coins. 'I didn't hear a thing.' He put the coins beside the empty plate, winked and left the eatery.

There was new-day warmth. At a dowdy shack at the far end of the village someone was warping a horse-shoe to fit, using an anvil.

An elderly soul was out front of the harness works adjusting a handmade shutter to his roadway window. His shop, and several others being on the west side of the road, caught morning sunlight. To someone who did close work with his hands too much light was troublesome.

The jailhouse looked to have been converted from one of those earlier buffalo hunter's cabins. It had four log walls and a roof of sugar pine shakes, the thick butt kind that didn't curl with age.

Out back, two saddle animals were standing shoulder to shoulder facing the back door of the jailhouse waiting to be fed.

A sprightly man who looked young came out of the shop to crank a barber pole so it would turn. He and Tug exchanged a nod and a smile. In the door of his shearing shop he hesitated. 'A dime, friend.'

Tug went up there. The barber was evidently also a metallurgist. There were gold scales atop an untidy desk.

As Tug settled to be shaved and shorn the younger man said, 'Passin' through or lookin' for work?'

'Visitin' is all,' Tug replied, thinking of the widow woman he'd known years back. He stalled further questioning by asking questions which the barber answered with the certainty of a man who not only knew his territory but quite a bit about its inhabitants.

Tug was looking out a window almost opposite the jailhouse when he said, 'You got a lawman?'

The reply came with a hint of pride. 'We're off a ways but we keep up with the times. We got a lawman. He does his job pretty well. In fact yestiddy he brought in a federal US marshal an' locked him up.'

'What for? US marshals — '

'Maybe not this one, friend. I heard last night it's a feller who lives sort of isolated south-west of town. I've sheared him a few times. Don't talk much. Has a half-grown son. Why they brought him in I haven't heard, but as far as I know there's no rule that says lawmen can't be outlaws too.'

Tug agreed. 'Yeah,' and waited until the haircutter and his interminable conversation ended, handed him a ten-cent coin and went out into the roadway.

Someone had fed the corralled horses out back. Tug crossed the road, considered a few chickens, a fat old dog and the few people who were abroad, tugged loose the tie-down over his 'borrowed' sixgun and walked to the little log structure, lifted the latch with his left hand, pulled the six-gun with his right hand and walked in.

The hefty individual sitting at the battered old desk looked up with widening eyes. He was motionless for as long as was required for Tug to kick the door closed at his back, then his gaze flicked to a shotgun someone had carelessly leaned aside and when Tug shook his head the lawman loosened a little.

Tug said, 'Where is he?'

The beefy man's reply was, 'Who?'

Tug crossed to the opposite side of the desk, cocked the pistol and said, 'You're runnin' out of time, 'possum belly. *Where is he!*'

The constable squirmed. 'Locked up.'

Tug gestured. 'Let's go unlock him.'

'Mister, you're makin' one hell of a bad mistake.'

'Get up, you fat son of a bitch!'

The constable arose.

'The key!' When the man opposite him leaned to open a desk drawer Tug also leaned. For several seconds they looked at each other before Tug said, 'Your left hand!'

The constable opened the top drawer slowly, picked up a key, closed the door and raised his eyes. 'You're goin' to get yourself killed. There's three fellers from down at Brighton rode in last night. They'll be along directly to take him back with 'em.'

Tug wigwagged with the cocked pistol. 'Lead the way.'

The cell had bars in front otherwise its three walls were log. The prisoner had been sitting on a wall bunk. He arose slowly.

As the constable unlocked the door and pushed it inward his prisoner wagged his head, shouldered past and left the cell.

When they were back up front he finally spoke to Tug. 'There's three fellers — '

'I know, 'possum belly told me.' Tug looked at the constable. 'Lead off to the alley doorway. *Move!*'

The burly constable moved. As he was opening the door, those eating horses out back briefly looked up then resumed eating.

Tug jammed the Colt barrel into the constable's back. 'Saddle that sorrel and bridle the buckskin.'

The constable obeyed. Under two sets of watchful eyes he left no slack in the cinch, but as he handed Tug the reins he said, 'You won't get five miles.'

Tug showed a humourless smile. 'You're goin' with us.' He handed the reins to Jeff's father, waited until he was astride then led the way to the end of the village, across the road to where he'd left his horse, got astride, holstered his six-gun and pointed. 'Constable, stay among the trees and start walkin'.'

The sun was climbing. Back in the village someone called a dog; the constable, red as a beet, walked ahead of the pair of mounted men. Once when he stopped, Tug asked him a question. 'Where are my saddle-bags?'

The perspiring constable answered sullenly. 'Where you'd never find 'em.'

Tug swung down, moved toward the heavier man and smiled as he swung a bony, rock-hard fist. The constable bent double, gasping. Tug stepped back. 'The saddle-bags!'

'Locked in . . . the safe at the . . . store.'

As Tug remounted he told his

prisoner to keep walking. When they came to a brushy clearing, Tug handed the marshal the six-gun. 'Mind him. If you got to, shoot him.'

'Where are you goin'?'

'Back for my saddle-bags.'

Walt shook his head. 'Not now, maybe tonight.'

'Just mind this son of a bitch,' Tug said, and turned back. Maybe the federal lawman was right but to Tug's way of thinking that contribution from the folk back at Brighton was going to set him up for the remainder of his life. He'd been lucky for a long time. Everyone runs out of luck sometime.

The sun was climbing, even among forest giants this near open country rising heat was noticeable. His horse jerked for slack, made one of his sideward swipes, got a mouthful of grass and dogged it along until Tug took up the slack, reined him down behind the village on the east side, dismounted and listened. There was no sound of particular interest until someone came out back to empty a basin of soiled water. It was Beth Holden. As she straightened up she looked around before going back inside and closing her alleyway door.

Walking into the village with an empty holster was bound to arouse interest. For a while that might be minimal, at least until the possemen from Brighton found that both the constable and his prisoner were gone.

He tethered the animal which immediately lowered its head to scarf up as much graze and brush as the tied reins allowed and ignored the two-legged thing hiking in the direction of the mud puddle caused when the café-woman emptied the pan.

If Beth Holden didn't have a gun he was going to be in trouble. For that matter if she had one he'd be in trouble — with her for wanting a gun.

He was no more than thirty feet from the doorway when she opened it ready to fling another pan of wash water when their eyes met.

She didn't move. She said, 'What are you doing out there, Tug?'

He grinned. 'Waiting for you.'

She twisted, flung the water, faced back with the empty pan at her side and frowned. Tug said, 'Can I come inside?'

Wordlessly she stepped aside and, after he had entered, she closed the door, looked steadily at him and spoke again.

'Tug, did you rob that store down south?'

'Yes ma'am, an' right now . . . someday I'll explain about that. Right now I need to know if you got a pistol.'

She didn't move. 'Where's yours?'

'I left it with a friend. Beth . . . ?'

'I'm not going to give you my gun. You're an outlaw, aren't you?'

Time was passing. He said, 'Beth, I got to have your gun.'

'There's nothing in this place worth stealing.'

'The gun, or do I have to ransack the place to find it? I'm not goin' to rob anyone.'

She finally moved, put the pan aside and passed him so close they brushed. Her six-gun was old. The blueing had been worn off it years earlier. She removed it from the drawer beneath her counter where it had been lying since the death of her husband — its previous owner — put it on the counter, glanced at the road and said, 'Half the folks in town know that gun by sight.'

He picked up the gun, holstered it, left the tiedown hanging loose and said, 'Much obliged. You won't get in any trouble. I promise you. Now, stay in here for a while. If you got some idea of huntin' up the constable to say I got your gun . . . ' He wagged his head.

Beth snapped at him, 'How can I find the law if I'm in here? Go out the back way, and Tug, if we ever meet again . . . never mind, just leave it.'

He left, studied the backs of adjoining buildings, saw no one, heard no commotion, the kind that would be raised when it was discovered the constable and his prisoner were missing, went cautiously toward the alleyway door of the general store, paused for a moment before grasping the door latch and lifting.

The scent inside was of sacked flour and sugar, vegetables and the kind of healthy mustiness that was common to mercantile establishments.

A man and two women were talking in the front of the store, one of those conversations common in stores. Tug listened, was satisfied the missing lawman and his prisoner had not as yet been discovered, otherwise in a drowsy village such as Bridgeport there would have been something other than a conversation concerning the cost of bolt goods womenfolk made clothing from.

When the female shoppers departed, a man with a bass voice came in for a sack of smoking tobacco and the brown papers that went with it from which cigarettes could be made.

That transaction didn't take long. Tug inched forward as far as an old drapery which closed off the storeroom where he was standing and the forward part of the store with its shelved goods and counter.

As Tug reached to part the drapery and draw Beth Holden's pistol, two boys came in and the ensuing transaction which concerned jaw breakers of different flavours took almost as long as it had taken for the earlier women shoppers to make purchases and depart.

Jaw breakers were marble-sized confections in a variety of tastes as well as colours. The reason the transaction took so long was because the boys had to make choices which involved the matter of different tastes.

The storekeeper was fortunately a patient man. It also helped that at the moment he had no other customers.

When the sale was finally consummated and the boys departed, Tug parted the drapery and got a surprise. The storekeeper was reaching to do the same thing. They were face to face from a distance of two feet.

The storekeeper froze with one arm still raised. In after years Tug did not believe he had ever seen an individual lose colour as quickly. The merchant was white to the hairline.

Tug raised and cocked the six-gun. 'Where's your safe, mister?'

The storeman finally lowered his arm but otherwise did not seem to even be breathing.

'Behind you in that little room where I store canned goods.'

'Let's go open it.'

The storekeeper did not make a sound. It required no great amount of intelligence for him to appreciate why the man with the gun wanted his safe opened. It was large, boxy and very heavy. It was decorated with dimpled cupids, badly faded but discernible.

Tug stood aside to watch his prisoner work the dial, which was as large as a fist. When the merchant leaned to haul back the door he spoke for the first time. 'I said I didn't want those bags of money in here. It'd be an invitation for someone — '

'Lift out the saddle-bags an' shut up.'

Tug slung the bags over one shoulder, herded the storekeeper to the alley with him, put the gun barrel against the other man's paunch and said, 'Fifteen minutes then you can holler your head off. Remember, fifteen minutes, or I'll come back and blow a hole in you.'

The merchant sank down on the stoop of his door. He didn't even watch Tug go swiftly in the direction of his saddle animal.

But someone else did, standing squarely in her doorway with hands on her hips.

She watched Tug get astride and go south until he broke over into a lope and was lost to sight among forest giants and their shadows.

6

Flight!

The constable and Walt Skinner were sitting on a deadfall log when Tug returned. He didn't dismount, he gestured for them to follow and led toward the coach road, crossed it and continued to skirt the logged-off area until he had big trees in all directions.

This far there had been no conversation. Where Tug halted he swung down, went to work using skirting thongs to make the saddle-bags fast to his saddle and when this was done he told the constable to sit down.

Walt dismounted. Tug ignored the federal marshal. He told the constable to shed his boots. They stared at each other until Tug said, 'Do it!'

The beefy lawman started to kick out of his boots. All three of them knew what would come next. For the constable it was a decidedly unpleasant prospect. His companions did not know it but he was very tender footed, had been all his life.

Tug jerked his head. 'Now walk back, 'possum belly,' and scooped up the constable's foot gear, mounted and didn't look back, but Walt Skinner did and the constable was still standing there.

They were riding in the direction of the Skinner place and Walt picked one of the rare wide places to get up beside Tug and say, 'That's where they'll head for.'

Tug nodded. 'We can't leave the boy.'

Skinner would have agreed with that but he was thinking beyond. 'Then what? They'll be fanning the country-side, not just the men from Brighton, everyone the constable can round up in Bridgeport. This'll end up bein' a real manhunt.'

Tug's preoccupation had been freeing Skinner and recovering his saddle-bags.

He hadn't thought much beyond those things and running for it.

He said, 'You got any ideas? I don't know the territory. How far's that squatter settlement you mentioned?'

'Half a day's ride,' the federal lawman replied and rode thoughtfully until they almost had his clearing in sight, then he spoke again. 'They'll eventually get over there, too. This country's sleepy, but rouse it up an' give 'em a reason an', mister, they won't let up.'

Tug did not comment. He saw Jeff come out of the barn and raised an arm. The boy recognized his father and ran to meet him. Tug understood. He'd once had a parent, but at the moment time and distance mattered. He told Jeff to saddle the buckskin and feed and water the horses while Tug and his father got supplies from the house.

The boy obeyed without a question. The fugitive outlaw had kept his word, he had freed the boy's father. For a while that would be enough.

Walt Skinner was a provident individual; he had stored tinned food against the fierce winters of the north country.

He and Tug half filled two croaker sacks, returned to the yard with them and met Jeff standing with his horse.

Walt gave the boy a fatherly slap on the shoulder, told him to get mounted and this time Walt led off riding westerly.

Just a half-good tracker would be able to read the sign as far as the Skinner cabin. Beyond that he would have to be better; even shod horses were difficult to track in country covered to a depth of about six inches with fir needles.

They rode in shadowy gloom, it slowed them but if the alternative had been open country it would have been worse.

The sun was high by the time they reached one of those little snowmelt creeks of cold water and stopped to let the horses drink. Tug's appropriated animal wasted only minutes tanking up at the creek. He was a stomach-oriented animal and did not stop cropping creek-side grass until Tug thought it was time to leave the creek.

Walt was swinging across leather when he said, 'We're better'n halfway,' and Tug responded with a question.

'You know any of these home-steaders?'

Walt knew them and they knew him. He did more shopping at their settlement than he did at Bridgeport. He had two reasons; one was he liked the people; the other reason was a buxom girl with pale eyes and flaxen hair.

Walt explained as much as he knew, up to this point, to his son. Jeff's reaction was almost enthusiastic. He had a few books. His favourite was the one entitled *Robin Hood And His Merry Men*.

He smiled broadly at his father without mentioning the dastardly Sheriff of Nottingham.

Walt did not smile. He had taken an

oath to uphold the law. He would not have helped Tug Carlyle if he'd known Tug was an outlaw. By the time he did know that it was too late and now he, too, was a wanted man.

He had ridden down his share of outlaws, knew the tricks and tactics of outlaws and rode in the lead in the direction of the squatter settlement thinking as outlaws thought, and one thing was a lead pipe cinch, the posse riders would visit the settlement in their tireless manhunt, and that worried him; where could they go beyond the settlement? The business of being hunted was a never-ending scramble to stay ahead.

The day was wearing along before they saw wisps of smoke rising above a clutch of log and slab houses near the wooden slopes.

Tug nodded; cattlemen settled in near the centre of their land, home-steaders settled clear of farmland.

They made their villages and towns in the unproductive areas. To them land that could be worked, made to produce should not be cluttered with roads and buildings. For them the idea was valid; to cattlemen, who were basically exploiters and indifferent, the rule was the opposite. They set up where there was water and shade, flat ground for buildings, corrals and fenced-yard pastures.

Jeff had been quiet the last few miles. Tug asked if he was worried and Jeff nodded. 'Mary Todd,' he said, 'I set out a pan of food and some water, but she can't walk very well.'

Tug had forgotten the wolf that had brought the three of them together. He said, 'We'll go back when we can,' and the youth looked at him.

'If we keep runnin' we won't get back before she runs out of grub and water.'

Jeff's father interrupted this discussion by raising an arm to point at a very large log house slightly apart from the others, near a sturdy log barn. The pole corral held four big, pudding-footed harness horses, twelve to fourteen hundred pound animals. He veered in that direction.

Jeff, riding beside Tug spoke quietly. 'That's Carl Freiberg's place. He farms northward for a considerable distance.' Jeff was briefly quiet. 'Pa'n Gretchen is friends.'

Tug accepted that, thinking they couldn't be very close friends with the distance that separated them.

Dusk hid the riders. Someone shouted and a dog barked. Tug saw the loose horse coming. Someone had forgotten to close a gate. It happened all the time. He reined clear of the Skinners, shook out his lariat, waited to see if the fleeing horse would stay on course and when it swung more northward Tug jumped out his mount, made a wide cast and took his dallies. The caught animal had been roped before. It stopped when the slack was taken up.

Jeff called to Tug. 'That was right good roping.'

They lined out down-slope where a

rawboned farmer was standing. Before they got close he said, 'Friend, I owe you. That danged animal can lift gate bars an' he's hard to catch.'

Tug handed the lariat to the raw-boned big farmer who led the way to his corral, turned the caught horse in and slammed the gate. Tug said, 'If you tied that gate bar to the bottom of the corral . . .'

The farmer used a catch-rope from a hip pocket. He used it to lash the latch to a bottom stringer of his corral, turned and said, 'We're fixin' to have supper. I'd take it kindly if you gents'd join us.'

They put their animals in another corral, an empty one, piled their outfits and while they were doing this the homesteader continued to express his gratitude until Walt turned from mounding his riding gear. When they faced each other the farmer said, 'Well, I'll be damned . . . Mr Skinner?'

They shook hands. Because the homesteaders originated in country where folks asked questions this one was blunt. 'You're a long way from home, Mr Skinner. You come over on business?'

Westerners did not ask personal questions. Walt Skinner was a transplant. He had no difficulty with the questioning except how to reply to it. He finally said, 'Came to see Carl,' and that satisfied the homesteader. He belonged to a community that thrived on gossip. It was common knowledge that when the federal lawman rode over and visited with the Freibergs, it was mostly with their daughter.

Jeff pitched hay to their horses and followed the others to the house, which had clearly been erected in a hurry by someone without much carpentry skill, but it was comfortable, a tad cramped, but comfortable.

The woman who opened the door was elderly, grey, lined, as sparsely built as a bird and moved about as quickly. She was the homesteader's mother. Her name was Eloise. The visitors addressed her as ma'am. Her last name was the same as her son's, Doyle, and she had a pleasant slight lilt when she spoke. Her husband had been killed in a cave-in. Her son, James, was all she had left this far from the Auld Sod.

Candles provided light and old Mother Doyle provided potatoes, coarse homemade bread, a huge pad of churned butter and a platter of elk haunch. Coffee was a luxury, spring water was a substitute.

While they were eating, the old woman made no attempt to describe her favoured treatment of Jeff. She didn't have to have a reason; the old and the young have a bond neither shares with people whose ages are between.

Someone rapped on the door. Walt, his boy and Tug jerked straight up. Beneath the table a six-gun cleared leather. The old woman opened the door and said, 'Carl!'

The man was large, muscular and solidly put together. 'I was at the barn, heard a running horse, went out to see an' three fellers was comin'. One of them roped the horse. It'd be your animal, that one that gets loose?'

Her son called from the table inviting the concerned man inside. He only advanced six feet when he saw Walt Skinner and stopped.

Walt arose, 'Passing through, Carl. This is my boy an' that's Tug Carlyle.'

The old woman brushed Freiberg's arm. 'Eat with us, Carl.'

He shook his head. 'Thanks all the same but supper's waiting me at home . . . Walt, good to see you.' Freiberg smiled at the elderly woman and turned toward the door. He hesitated, looking back. Walt left the table to follow Freiberg out into the night.

Tug's appetite was gone. He had eaten his full anyway. He asked the homesteader questions about the settlement, the north and westerly country beyond, absorbed what he was told, winked at Jeff and arose.

The old woman surprised him. 'Light

up inside, Mr Carlyle.'

She fished forth a corncob pipe. 'I'll join you.'

When Walt returned, Tug methodically rolled and lighted a brown-paper cigarette. Walt gazed at Tug and said, 'We can lie over a few days. Carl needs a couple of swathers to help with haying.'

The idea had little appeal to Tug. Two days was a healthy head start. He didn't relish the idea of wasting it until Skinner also said, 'They'll watch northward. There's no love lost between these folks and the folks around Brighton.'

Tug nodded non-committally. For a fact he and his borrowed horse needed a rest, but as sure as the Lord had made green apples the manhunters would come this far. Whether they could read sign or not they knew where this place was; they might even know Skinner came over here. He said, 'Let's sleep on it,' and went outside to check on that corral gate and their three mounts who seemed well enough off to sleep in their customary way, standing up and hip-shot.

Walt came soundlessly, also looked at the animals and spoke without looking around. 'These folks got no use for Ames Felton. They got even less use for stockmen posse riders. Some of them've been burnt out. Stockmen used this flat country for springtime graze for years. Ranchers can't do much any more. There's too many homesteaders, but they would if they could.'

Tug leaned on the peeled-pole stringers. 'Walt, it's been my experience that as long as a man can stay ahead he's got a chance, stoppin' costs a man his headway.'

The woman came out of darkness as soundlessly as a mouse. Even by poor light she was handsome. She ignored Tug. 'Walt?'

As he turned, Tug had a glimpse of his face and its expression. If he figured to keep running from here on he'd do it alone.

Walt and the girl walked off into the darkness leaving Tug to ponder. If there was an alternative to flight he didn't find it. Something troubled him mildly; he had no family except for the brother he'd never been able to find, and for that reason, along with the basic one of all outlaws — lack of attachments — he should have had no difficulty; while the others slept this night he would continue his flight.

The mildly troubling thing was how Walt Skinner had done what he could to keep Tug a free man, and the boy with his shy smile, uncommon wisdom for a fourteen-year-old and the closeness among the three of them.

He rolled and lighted a smoke. For the first time since he could remember he wished strongly that things could have been different. But it was too late to dwell on that.

He killed the smoke, got his bedroll, went in the opposite direction Walt had taken and prepared to bed down until the village was dark with slumbering people.

His forever-hungry young horse had 'bottom'. All horses in their prime had endurance, some more than others. Tug's big thoroughbred had it. As he dropped down on his unrolled soogan and looked straight up he told himself he would come back when he could, find his horse and the two of them would continue their odyssey. That thought prompted another: how long can a man outsmart his enemies? Common sense implied that down the road of every fleeing fugitive there was an end to the trail.

He had his saddle-bags; this time he would continue to ride until he found a place to settle. After that he would turn over the leaf he probably should have turned over some years earlier.

He had no idea when he fell asleep nor how long he had slept when someone roughly shook him. Walt was leaning over. 'Jeff's gone.'

Tug sat up scratching, groped for his

hat, dumped it on and said, 'When?'

'Sometime last night. Him and the buckskin are gone.'

Tug stopped scratching. The two men looked steadily at each other with the same thought. Tug said, 'Mary Todd?' and as Walt stepped aside so Tug could stand up he nodded. 'Only reason I can think of.'

Tug knelt to roll his soogans. As he lashed the bindings he said, 'Y'know, Walt, once when I was younger'n Jeff I found a starved, abandoned puppy.' Tug arose and gave the bedroll a light kick before continuing. 'That little dog'n me had a lot in common. I took it with me, fed it an' when it was three years old I found some folks who wanted it. They'd take good care of it.' Tug looked easterly. There was no brightening sky over there but there would be. He looked back. 'We're goin' to need one hell of a lot of luck. The woods back yonder'll be crawlin' with possemen.'

As they returned to the corral, Walt said, 'You don't have to do this.'

112

Tug smiled. 'Some of the things I've done the last few years I didn't have to do, but I did 'em anyway. Let down that gate bar.'

Except for a dog, evidently a light sleeper, no light appeared as they led the animals out to be saddled.

It was chilly, but like the Irishman who died and went to Hell didn't mind the heat he was so busy shaking hands with old friends, neither Tug nor Walt noticed the chill.

When they breasted the topout and began the interminable dodging and weaving among big old trees Walt said, 'Dang that kid anyway.'

Tug thought of his puppy. 'Walt, I got an idea that girls always got to have somethin' to love; maybe that goes for boys, too.'

Even after dawn came they were unable to make good time. They startled some elk and further along a ragged-eared old boar bear working strenuously at tearing bark off a bee tree. They gave that area a wide berth.

They didn't encounter any bees; they were probably fully engaged attacking the bear.

It was a long ride. The sun came but horsemen in a forest rarely saw even shafts of light. Tug took the shortest route. He had no illusions; if they didn't meet manhunters it would be a genuine miracle. Under these circumstances he was disinclined to believe a miracle would occur, and he was right.

They didn't see riders but they heard them northward, clearly following the earlier tracks in the direction of the squatter settlement.

Tug dropped slightly more southerly. They had covered about two-thirds of the distance when someone northward let go a loud shout followed by several clearly distinguishable words.

'Down here, goin' back!'

Tug shook his head, let the tie-down over his holster hang loose and when Walt spoke he told him sound carried. Walt did not speak again.

Ahead where it was possible to see

where the trees thinned out Tug rode erectly. If the manhunters who were now following their fresh tracks were coming in behind them, all they'd need would be for other riders to be coming from the east in the direction Tug and Walt were riding.

They were. In fact Tug hissed and raised a hand. Through the trees he saw three men moving northerly across his line of sight.

They sat motionless until the manhunters had passed well along.

Tug reined his mount to its slowest walk which was not as simple as it should have been; the young horse was in the habit of stepping out and tossed its head at being restrained.

About the time they had the clearing with its log buildings in sight someone shouted again. This time an unmistakable sound of triumph in his voice.

'Headin' for the cabin, Ames!'

That statement settled the question concerning who the closing-in possemen were. At least they knew who one of them was: Ames Felton, the constable.

Tug had a moment to wonder why Felton wasn't with that other, larger group riding toward the settlement.

He would have an answer after he and Walt halted among the thinned-out trees to look in the direction of the clearing and a quiet voice said, 'Don't move! Keep your hands where I can see 'em! Now then, shuck them guns — use your left hand, gents!'

7

Freed a Second Time

He was alone and evidently on foot, at least there was no horse in sight. Tug thought he looked vaguely familiar but didn't make a connection until he moved from behind a big tree, held his cocked six-gun in a steady hand and walked over, looked down and exclaimed, 'Well I'll be damned. That's my gun.' As he bent to retrieve the Colt, Tug removed his right foot from the stirrup. The gunman looked up. 'Your leg isn't long enough!'

He was right but desperate men do desperate things. Tug couldn't have kicked their captor in the head by six or eight inches.

He wigwagged with the cocked gun. 'Get down! Now then lead them horses toward the house. Get cute an' I'll kill you!'

His prisoners dismounted and began walking. There wasn't a sound until they cleared the trees and a horse the walking man could not see, trumpeted. He had evidently caught the scent of the led horses.

Two men emerged from the house. One held a carbine in the crook of his arm. They stood like statues watching Tug and Walt walking ahead of their captor. One of them said something indistinguishable to the prisoners and his companion started hurriedly toward the barn, his purpose obvious: to find the other manhunters and bring them back.

Constable Felton was chewing a blade of grass. He watched the procession from an expressionless face until there was no doubt about the identity of the captives, then he spat out the grass and smiled. If a man ever deserved a feather in his hat it was he, because he had caught a US federal marshal turned renegade.

Jeff appeared in the doorway, stone-faced and mute until he was snarled at then he passed from sight inside the house.

The man who had caught them let go a rattling noisy sigh, herded his prisoners to the house and stopped them. The only sound for a long moment was of the departing posseman riding in a lope in the direction of the timber.

The constable looked longest at Tug. The humiliation at being responsible for losing a prisoner rankled. He said, 'You son of a bitch, we're goin' to hang the pair of you. Where's them saddle-bags?'

Tug twisted toward his saddle without speaking. Felton followed that line of sight and had a slight change of attitude but his rancour lingered. 'There's three fellers from Brighton with us. They want you real bad. They counted the money yestiddy an' it was five hunnert dollars short.'

Tug spoke for the first time. 'How's the boy?'

'Got hit a little, otherwise he's fine. Had a shotgun when we rode in. He's got a damned bitch wolf inside with a busted leg.'

Walt said, 'You hit him, Ames?'

'Onliest way I could get the shotgun from him.' The constable smiled at Skinner. 'Good thing you don't keep 'em loaded in the house.'

Tug said, 'If you're goin' to take us in, let's get going.'

The beefy man made a humourless small grin. 'We'll just wait until those boys from Brighton get here. Mister, they want you real bad. You shot a man down there.'

It could have been true but it wasn't likely; random firing from the hurricane deck of a running horse was almost a guarantee a shooter couldn't hit the side of a barn.

Felton took the captives into the house. The man who had made the capture and another man Tug did not

120

recognize also came inside.

Jeff was kneeling with his bitch wolf. Both pans he had left were empty. Jeff was watering her from a third pan. She paused drinking long enough to look up and wag her tail at Walt and Tug.

The constable said, 'Might as well shoot her, boy. Put her out of her misery.'

When Jeff raised his head Tug and Walt saw the smashed mouth and the blood. Tug instinctively threw out an arm to stop Jeff's father. One of the men near the door said, 'Let him go', with unmistakable meaning and Constable Felton nodded agreement.

He aimed a kick. Jeff blocked it with an out-flung arm. The wolf ignored them both; she was thirsty. Dry jerky did that whether it was a four-legged or a two-legged animal that ate it.

A man arrived out front on a lathered horse. He didn't bother to loop the reins. He swung off and burst into the house brushing aside the man standing close.

He had narrowed eyes and a bloodless slit of a mouth. He looked steadily at the only unarmed men in the room. Ames Felton said, 'That's them, Constable.'

The rawboned, lanky newcomer continued to glare as he addressed Felton. 'You want me to sign a paper or somethin' before I take 'em back to Brighton?'

Constable Felton wasn't quite ready to hand over his prisoners. 'Directly,' he said. 'Gents, this here is the constable from Brighton, Frank Kellogg. Mister Kellogg, that one there is a deputy US marshal. That one's the feller who done the damage down at Brighton. His name's Tug Carlyle.'

Other riders appeared in the yard, noisily and in haste. To Tug and Walt it didn't seem possible that they could have gone more than maybe a third of the way toward the homesteader settlement to have returned so quickly.

There wasn't room in the parlour so these riders remained in the doorway.

One of them Tug recognized, he was one of the men who had come with Constable Felton on his first visit.

His right cheek was swollen with a cud of molasses cured tobacco. He addressed no one in particular when he said, 'Is there a bounty on 'em?'

No one answered, this was not the time for practical considerations. Tug worried; lynch talk would have worried a cigar-store Indian.

Walt regarded Felton from an expressionless face with murderous eyes.

The lawman from Brighton said, 'Let's go with this,' and led the way outdoors. He and Ames Felton had been cut from widely different strips of cloth. Frank Kellogg was a no-nonsense individual. He went after his horse without looking around. He was joined there by his two companions from Brighton; one was barely old enough to shave; the other one was fleshy with the kind of fair complexion that went with saloon keepers, which is what he did for a living, ran Brighton's liquor dispensing water-hole.

Departure from the Skinner place was made by an untidy straggling band of riders several of whom had barely got back to the yard before the exodus commenced.

Constable Kellogg rode on one side of the prisoners. On the other side was that stringy, weathered rangeman who had been at the Skinner place some days back with Ames Felton. They both rode in silence. The rangeman occasionally considered the prisoners. The posse rider from Brighton did not once turn his head. Like his manhunting companions from down yonder, his mood was murderous.

Ames Felton set both the pace and the direction. They had left Jeff back with his injured animal. The last thing Felton said to the boy was that he'd do better to shoot that damned bitch wolf.

There was little conversation but not up where the prisoners were and it was both inconsequential and sporadic.

Felton aimed downward to the coach

road and turned north. He led all the way. It was consistent with his nature to appear as the leader.

Bridgeport knew they were coming. It was the only band of horsemen in sight.

People watched, silent and expressionless. Beth Holden studied riders pass from her roadway front window. She bit her lower lip at the sight of Tug Carlyle's empty holster and erect bearing, looking neither right nor left.

At the jailhouse the local men scattered. The men from Brighton trooped inside. One, the pus-gutted saloonman, went directly to a hanging canteen and drank.

Frank Kellogg's reply to Felton's action of reaching for his ring of keys was curt. 'We'll eat then come for 'em.' Kellogg led the exodus of his companions leaving behind two Bridgeport residents and their constable.

Felton sank down at his old desk. He had never liked posse riding, his feet ached and he felt tired although the day was still young. He tossed a key to one of his companions and jerked his head. The keyholder jerked his head for Tug and Walt to follow. For Walt, being returned to the jailhouse's only cell was not exactly pleasant; for Tug Carlyle, who had never been in the cell before, it was different. He perched on the wall bunk, leaned his back against the wall and considered his companion.

Walt said, 'I've put my share in these things. If someone'd bet me a hunnert dollars I'd end up in one I'd've laughed in his face,' and followed Tug's example of sitting on a bunk.

Tug gazed at the seated man. 'It's not anythin' I'd laugh about. But if you want to bet, how much would you put up that we never reach Brighton?'

Walt considered the toes of his boots in long silence.

In the office they could hear men talking, not loudly enough for words to be distinguished but talking nonetheless.

Time passed; more than enough time

for the Brighton possemen to have eaten and no one came to the cell room.

Tug was faintly scowling. 'Maybe they figure to hang us in Bridgeport instead of down yonder. It's sure quiet out there.'

Eventually one voice was distinguishable, not because it was loud but because it had a higher pitch. Tug went to lean on the cell's front. Walt said, 'Who in hell is that?'

Tug's reply was to himself. 'She's goin' to get herself killed. Half this damned town's for a lynching.'

'What? Who are you . . . who is she?'

Instead of replying Tug pressed closer to catch every word. He loosened slightly when a chair squeaked and a door was opened.

Constable Felton appeared first, red as a beet, the tie-down hanging loose over his empty holster. Behind was Beth Holden.

Walt came up to his feet. He knew the café-woman, not well but by sight.

He'd eaten at her place a few times.

His mouth was hanging open.

The constable leaned to unlock the cell. As he straightened back he said, 'Beth; you'll never get away with it. Those fellers from Brighton'll be along directly. You're goin' to get yourself shot.'

Her answer stunned both prisoners. 'They're locked in my storeroom. Get back. Stand away from the door. Tug . . . ?'

He left the cell with Walt behind him. Once Walt looked from one of them to the other. They tied and gagged the constable and left him locked in the cell they had just been in.

Beth herded them to the back alley door and outside where a reddening sun was listing toward the west. She let the gun sag briefly before handing it to Tug. 'Get on your horses and don't even stop . . . Tug?'

He leaned, kissed her cheek, leathered the constable's weapon and left. Walt knew Bridgeport from one end to the other. There was no livery barn but, as was customary, there was a small network of corrals.

Tug hesitated. 'Beth . . . ?'

'I'll be all right. They wouldn't lynch a woman.'

Tug's reply was curt. 'Yes, they will. Come along.'

'I don't have a horse.'

Tug took her by the arm and pulled. They followed Walt to the public corral where Tug got a pleasant surprise. His bay thoroughbred was scarfing up the last stalks of a flake of hay. He hadn't just been shod on his tender foot, he had been shod all around. It would be a long time before Tug understood the reason for that. Ames Felton had claimed the horse for feeding him. He'd had him shod by a local rangeman who augmented his twelve dollars a month wage by shoeing horses in his spare time. He wasn't as good a horseshoer as he might have been; he used cold shoes exclusively. Tug's thoroughbred was one of those animals with good feet: he could get by with cold shoeing.

Two women and an old man appeared. The women had been in process of hanging wet wash over a rope. The second woman handed up things to be draped from a large wicker basket.

The old man had been taking a daily walk with a knob-headed cane. He had heard walking would keep his legs spry. It was a damned lie. He'd been walking for six months and he still couldn't step over a two by four.

He showed no particular interest in two men and a woman rigging out horses until they began rigging out a solidly built sorrel mare with a flaxen mane and tail. Then he perked up. The sorrel mare belonged to his son, the Bridgeport storekeeper. She was a combination horse, broke both to ride and drive. Storekeepers ordinarily owned that kind of animal to help with the delivery business.

The old gummer stamped up to the outside of the corral and said, 'What'n hell you think you're doin'? That's my boy's horse.'

He was ignored. Beth got astride. Women who wore skirts had difficulty maintaining modesty and the old gaffer wasn't *that* old. He didn't say another word as his son's big mare followed the other two horses out of the corral. Only when they veered northward did the old man loudly squawk.

The pair of laundresses left their work and hastened to find their husbands.

Walt knew the country. He pushed into a lope for almost a mile then abruptly veered eastward. Tug would have bet his horse Walt would have turned westerly which was the direction they'd find his son.

Beth's big mare did a creditable job of keeping up. In fact she was accustomed to being ridden into rough country. Her owner was an avid buck hunter.

Beth was uncomfortable, not especially about undue exposure; she hadn't been on a saddle horse in ten years and this one had a back as broad as a barrel.

Tug had to be satisfied Walt knew where he was going. It was not misplaced confidence. They worked their way among trees for over an hour before they came to what appeared to be a dead end; not only because they were faced by a massive cliff face but also because bypassing this rugged country looked to be either impossible or likely to waste time trying to find a way around.

A lively little creek with flourishing growth on both sides provided water for sweating animals. Walt dismounted, slipped the bridle, looped reins around the animal's neck and watched his companions alight. To Tug, Walt did not look worried about the impassivity of the straight-up rock face yards from the creek.

When everyone had tanked up, Walt jerked his head and led his horse. Tug and Beth Holden dutifully followed. The only difficulty they encountered was a tangled mass of prickly weeds intermingled with ripgut grass and several flourishing but scrubby trees with branches extending in all directions making Walt's progress uncomfortable.

Beyond the natural barrier, Walt led through a wide crevice at the base of the cliff, wide enough for a horse to pass, probably what remained of a prehistoric water-course. It was shadowy with several trees part way along. Squeezing around them was slow work.

The distance was several hundred feet. It was cool in this hidden place with a rough stone ceiling well above the height of those passing along.

Walt eventually halted. He was standing partly in slanting sunshine. He looked back, was satisfied and pushed the last yard or so into a clearing of respectable size. Some time, probably aeons earlier, hunter-gatherers had lived in this secret place. There were somewhat disturbed rings of rocks — tipi rings.

Tug stood with his leggy bay horse making a slow examination of this place.

Walt led almost to the middle where deer and elk had trampled the grass, flung up his left saddle *rosadero*, tugged loose the cinch and dumped his riding gear. For the first time Tug spoke.

'How'd you find this place?'

'Jeff found it coupla years back. He's hell to go exploring.'

Beth Holden unsaddled, looked for hobbles that weren't there and turned loose the 1,100 pound combination animal anyway. The other horses were eating. The big mare found a suitable spot, went down on front legs, kicked loose with the hind one and rolled over and back three times before arising and shaking, then she went to grazing. Tug thought hobbled or not she wouldn't stray far from the other two horses and he was right; mares were more likely to form attachments and stay with companions than geldings.

Walt led off toward the far side of the meadow. Where he stopped there were four stone mounds, what later generations called 'Greek ovens', carefully mounded stones. Centuries of use and subsequent centuries of disuse had not done much to obliterate the dark burned place where cooking had been done. As he was gazing at these things he said, 'From over here they could see the place you had to come through.'

Tug nodded. There had probably always been that tangle of dense, tall brush back yonder, and maybe even trees.

Beth studied the Greek ovens with the look of an experienced cook. She said, 'They'll do well enough. The question is what do we cook?'

Tug grinned. He knew something about the streak of practicality in female women. His answer was simply given. 'We'll find somethin', the question is how long can we hide here? We left tracks. In my case shod-horse tracks.'

Walt batted at a flying insect. 'Overnight,' he said. 'I don't know of another place like this. If there was one Jeff would have found it . . . I worry about them going back where Jeff is. I owe that 'possum-bellied son of a bitch for striking my boy.'

Tug was not especially hungry but he was tired. Neither he nor Walt had slept since they'd been fed at the squatter settlement.

Tug made a bed in a shady spot and would have slept away what was left of the day if annoying mosquitos hadn't driven him to using his ground cloth to hide under.

Beth and Walt sat by a little twig fire and talked until they too succumbed. Walt made a decent sleeping place for the woman with two of the blankets he stole from Tug, stamped the ground to flatten and also to scatter any crawling varmints that might be in it and when Beth asked how he would sleep, told her he'd slept on trampled grass many years. Her next question caught Walt

136

unprepared. 'How well do you know Tug Carlyle?'

'Well, I guess as well as a man has to when someone helps his kid. I guess you knew I'm a deputy US marshal.'

She knew. In a place no larger than Bridgeport if a person wanted to keep a secret the best way was to tell it first.

Walt also had a question. 'Why'd you do that?'

She understood and faintly smiled. 'I knew Tug years back. I didn't believe he was an outlaw.'

'Well, ma'am, he is.'

Her soft smile widened as she considered Walt Skinner. 'An outlaw and a federal lawman together?'

He grinned. 'It's a long story. You better get some sleep.'

8

A Secret Place

Dawn had to reach over the big cliff to reach the secret small meadow. The horses had been eating for several hours; the big sorrel mare had never thought of leaving the other horses.

Tug met Walt at the creek, both grunted and went to work making themselves as presentable as was possible under the circumstances and although neither would have mentioned it, with the woman close by they ran bent fingers through their hair a few extra licks.

Tug scouted up a way to get atop the bluff. The two people he left behind did their best to rassle a meal of jerky and creek water. It wouldn't be anything folks would want to live on for long but it beat hell out of being embarrassed by stomach rumbles.

Beth asked more questions, some of which Walt could not answer, his acquaintanceship with the fugitive hadn't been very long.

Eventually he reared back on his heels and asked a question of his own. 'If you knew him years back . . . ?'

She kept her head averted to hide the rising colour. 'It'd been so long I thought we'd never meet again. He was a decent man.'

She faced Walt. 'Ames Felton is a pig. You want to know how I got his gun?'

Walt nodded.

'He's been tryin' to feed the cow to get the calf a long time. One time some months back he came to the café when no one else was around an' grabbed me. He was going to kiss me. I hit him in the gut. Since then he hasn't got real close, but I could count on it; he eats at the counter regular an' makes sly remarks.

'I watched those men from Brighton leave the jailhouse. They made a beeline for my eatery. When they were eatin' I used an old scattergun to herd them to the storeroom and barred the door from the outside.

'Then I went over to the jailhouse, smiled at Ames, went around his desk and sat on his lap. He got all excited. I leaned past, yanked loose the tie-down, shoved the gun into his belly and you know the rest.'

'Except for one thing,' stated Walt. 'Folks don't do things that could get 'em killed except they got a good reason . . . you?'

'I already told you, we were friends years back.'

Walt understood this was the only answer he was going to get so he made no further attempt to keep their conversation going.

When Tug returned, Beth fed him, laughed at his expression after the first mouthful and asked him if this situation reminded him of anything. Tug chewed, eventually swallowed and shook his head.

She persevered. 'That *Cinco de Mayo* barbecue down near Adelanto five, six years back.'

He looked, eyes widening. 'You was one of the women at the pits.'

She nodded. 'And I brought you a platter after you won the horseshoe-pitching match.'

He smiled. 'It's hard to make goat meat tough but you ladies at the grill sure did.'

Walt interrupted. 'See anything up yonder?'

Tug's attention went to Walt. 'They're fanned out but south of here.'

Walt growled. 'Goin' west like yesterday. They'll figure we'll be at the cabin.'

Beth said, 'Where will we be? Maybe they're also combing the upcountry with trackers.'

Walt arose without speaking, went after his horse and had to wait until his companions also got rigged out. Then he said, 'You two head north. There's a town about forty miles with a railroad

siding. Eat hearty and keep goin'
north.'

Tug was softly frowning when he
said, 'An' you?'

'If that son of a bitch hits my boy
again I want to be there.'

Tug trickled a long breath. 'You,
alone against maybe six, eight or ten of
'em?'

'Nobody hits Jeff. I owe Ames for
hittin' him before.'

Tug had learned early about stub-
born people. It wasn't just the set of the
jaw it was the undeviatingly wintry look
in the eyes.

He faced Beth. 'You could stay hid
until we come back.'

Before she could speak, Walt glared at
Tug. 'This time you stay out of it,' and
got an equally unrelenting glare from
the outlaw.

'Sometimes, Walt, you talk too much.
Get on your horse!' Oddly enough for a
female Beth did not say a word as she
watched them ride toward the prehistoric waterless waterway.

Walt said, 'They'll be around like fleas on a dog,' and Tug's reply was dryly given.

'You know why lawmen don't catch outlaws? Because outlaws work accordin' to a real simple rule: stay ahead. Always stay ahead an' the law will always be behind you.'

Walt knew the country and whether his companion's philosophy was right or not, Walt knew something about fugitives and manhunters.

Without a word he made for high places. Once they found a very old fire ring. The view from this high place was perfect; in every direction it was possible to see movement. Trees were an obstacle but the early-day tomahawks, like the lawman and his outlaw companion, had all the time they would need. Any movement, but especially mounted men would eventually be seen.

With their animals far enough back to be unseen from below, the two hunted men, who were now both fugitives, squatted as the prehistoric hunters and gatherers had done, tipped hatbrims forward, and watched.

Walt was especially interested in the south-westerly distance: the direction of his cabin and his son.

This time it wasn't just the Bridgeport constable and his friends; this time there were at least eight or ten riders searching for them.

Walt was watching a scorched small clearing where a lightning strike had killed trees so that daylight showed through, when he said, 'Tug! That old burn!'

The distance made a pair of horsemen appear half size but there was no mistaking their purpose; they rode apart, occasionally standing in their stirrups and sunlight reflected off steel butt plates of booted carbines.

Tug said, 'Son of a bitch! They're behind us.'

That bothered his companion less than the angling course of the riders. They were coming from the north-west angling in the direction of his clearing and its log house.

Tug looked at Walt who was getting to his feet as the manhunters passed from sight into the forest. Tug said, 'This time it's not goin' to be them huntin' us. We'll be huntin' them an', Walt, they'll most likely be thickest around your place.' As Tug also arose looking in the direction the distant riders had taken, he also said, 'Like it or not, partner, we got to wait for dark.'

The logic was sound but the expression on Walt's face made Tug swear under his breath. Walt was already going back to the horses.

Tug sighed as he followed. Walt did not even look at his companion as he reined down-slope and worked his way among trees on a westerly course.

Tug guessed Walt's idea. Two hours later his surmise turned out to be correct. Walt wasn't heading straight for the cabin, he was riding westerly to get behind the country of his home.

The forest shadows that reflected

afternoon sunlight back upward from stiff treetops were beginning to deepen and lengthen.

Walt altered course, but did it in a wide sashay. They were riding southward, Tug almost smiled. For a lawman, Walt Skinner was showing the *coyote* traits of a seasoned fugitive. It wasn't a sighting that heightened their caution, it was the trumpeting of a horse and for the first time Walt looked around smiling. 'That came from the salt-lick area,' he said, and again changed course.

Tug was worried. They had to be close enough to the cabin to have manhunters behind them. The forest gloom was some protection, but he knew from experience that manhunters watched for movement and if they had been seen, their direction known, somewhere up ahead there was an ambush.

He freed the tie-down thong, alternately peered ahead and speculated where the ambush would occur.

It didn't. They came out atop a heavily forested spit of land where visibility was excellent. There were no tethered animals in his clearing. Tug jutted his jaw. 'In the barn. If we ride in down there . . . '

'We won't walk into their trap,' Walt said, and rode almost due southward. He did this with brief intervals for looking and listening.

Tug softly said, 'They're around,' and got back a cryptic comment. 'Another half-mile.'

Tug tested the air, moved his eyes constantly and was beginning to wonder when Walt twisted, gestured in the direction of stands of trees riders would be unable to penetrate and would have to ride around.

Walt swung off and led his horse. As Tug followed this example he wondered what in hell his companion was doing. If he expected to hide in those trees . . .

Walt stopped. It was difficult to see more than thirty feet ahead. The only signal Tug got was how the huge old close-spaced forest giants seemed to be unusually tall for big trees. He had an answer when Walt led off slightly southerly then looped his reins over a low branch, held a finger to his lips and started walking.

The reason those tall trees seemed unusually tall was because the land gently sloped upwards, something difficult to ascertain in a territory where it was hard to see ahead fifty feet.

The rise was gradual. It wasn't rocky as much as it seemed to be sandstone. At least it was that colour.

Tug got his first surprise when they made out two dozing horses tied a few feet apart.

Walt stopped. When Tug came up Walt leaned to softly say, 'Just beyond those buck brushes there's an old cave.'

They continued walking until Tug saw the opening. For height it was about right for a bear den, for width it was wider.

They reached the east side of the

cave and halted again. There wasn't a sound coming from inside the cave. Walt stiffened and twisted; if no one was in there then they had to maybe be scouting the area on foot.

Walt brushed Tug's sleeve, palmed his six-gun and walked the last fifteen or twenty feet where they flattened against the easterly side of the hole to listen.

What Tug heard was uneven, rattling snoring. Walt's expression lightened slightly. He stepped into the opening, pistol high and waited just long enough for his eyes to become adjusted to the gloom, then went foward in a slight crouch.

The old den had a relatively high ceiling for a bear den but anyone above less than average height had to stoop a little.

There were two of them sprawled atop an ancient assortment of bedding made of twigs and brittle, long dead grass.

One was lying on his back, his

companion was on his left side, one arm out-flung.

Walt leaned to remove the nearest sleeper's sidearm and was stepping over to do the same to the second man when the first one moved, shifted position and sat up rubbing his eyes.

He stopped stone still. Two armed men with weapons in their hands were spitting close.

He seemed almost to have lost the ability to breathe. Tug put a finger to his lips until Walt had lifted away the second sleeper's six-gun.

Walt bunted the second man with a boot toe. The only reaction he got was a half cough-half groan. He knelt, pushed the gun he had just appropriated into the ear of the sound sleeper. That got a reaction, but not immediately, not until the sleeper brushed the side of his face to rid himself of what he probably thought was a crawling creature.

His fingers touching the gun barrel brought his eyes wide open.

Tug smiled at him. Walt neither

smiled nor spoke. The second man saw Tug standing near his feet with a six-gun in his hand and turned to stone.

Walt broke the hush. 'Who are you?'

The man with the gun in his ear seemed to have lost the ability to speak. His companion answered for him.

'We're posse riders with Ames Felton from Bridgeport. We was in the village for supplies. We work for Downing's Big Tree cow outfit.' The speaker paused, sat up, looked over where his companion moved only his eyes, looked up at Tug and said, 'You'll be them fellers we're lookin' for?'

Tug restrained an urge to laugh. Ranch hands, while commonly dragooned to ride as possemen, were, as these two seemed to be, something less than two-legged bloodhounds.

Tug addressed the man nearest him. 'Where are the others?'

The cowboy gestured. 'Scattered around, some at that cabin, the others foragin' the area.'

Walt stood up. The man on the ground reached with one hand to massage his ear. He considered the pair of fugitives and said, 'Truth is, gents, we put in a rough night last night, found this cave and come in here.' The cowboy paused before also pensively saying, 'They're beatin' the brush all around for you gents. Constable Felton's put a price, twenty-five dollars for you dead or alive.'

The man facing Tug got a furrowed brow and addressed Walt. 'Ain't you that fed'ral marshal folks know in Bridgeport?'

Walt leathered his weapon before replying. He didn't smile but he clearly felt relieved. These two possemen wouldn't be a danger even if their positions had been reversed. He ignored the question to ask one of his own. 'You been to my house down yonder?'

The ear-massaging man answered. 'We was there. Constable Felton told us you'd come back here for your boy.

There's three fellers from down at Brighton. They want to hang you.' The rangeman leaned to arise. Walt growled and the man sank back down.

His companion said, 'Did one of you fellers really get away with three thousand dollars from down yonder?'

That question was left hanging as Walt told the rangemen to empty their pockets. They both protested that they did not own belly-guns and got to their knees to empty their pockets. He was right, there were clasp knives, coins, a few crumpled greenbacks and little else. As the man who had asked about $3,000 was straightening up he addressed Tug. 'It's a heap of money, mister, if you can get away an' keep it.'

Tug nodded agreement without speaking.

Walt asked questions some of which the captives could not answer but the ones they could answer helped Walt decide the future.

He and Tug had arrived simulta- neously at the same notion. These two were rangemen who'd joined a posse for the pay, one dollar a day. They were not dangerous. The problem was what to do with them. The most talkative of the pair was looking at Tug when he said, 'Three thousand dollars, for Chris'sake,' and wagged his head.

Tug fished in a pocket, brought forth a pad of money and said, 'How much was the constable goin' to pay you gents?'

The answer came quickly; brilliant the cowhands might not be but it didn't require brilliance to guess what that question being asked by the man with a folded pad of greenbacks was leading to.

The sullen man eyed the money, looked at his companion and replied to Tug. 'Twenty dollars, mister. We were fixin' to leave for Texas anyway.'

Tug sorted out notes, handed each man twenty dollars and accompanied that with a promise.

'If you get cute, mister, I'll hunt you down and kill you. Stand up!'

Walt's expression showed scepticism but he said nothing. The talkative man held out his hand. 'That gun cost me four dollars.'

Tug retrieved both weapons, punched them empty and handed them to their owners. He had one more question. 'How'd you find this cave?'

The sullen man answered as he was arising. His tone was different. 'We was scoutin' an' come on to a cow elk lookin' for a place to calve. She run through the trees. We followed until we lost her and there was this bear den.' He was pocketing money when he also said, 'It's been used lately. The bear stink is in here.'

The pair of rangemen led off southward from the cave. They had left their horses tied among trees and underbrush. As they were snugging up before mounting, Walt said, 'Due south an' don't look back.'

The rumpled, unshaven pair got astride and the talkative one nodded as he followed his friend.

Tug sighed. 'They won't come back.'

Walt might have agreed but he had turned to go back for their own mounts. Whether the itinerant rangemen returned or not Walt was thinking ahead.

They were less than a half-mile from his clearing, close enough to smell smoke from a cook stove. As they stopped to look below, a man rode into the yard on a tired horse, put his animal out of sight in the barn and crossed to the house.

The day was wearing along. It was Tug's guess other searchers on tired horses would be arriving. This time when they rode, Tug took the lead. Walt followed without comment. He understood; the outlaw-fugitive part of his companion knew more about what they had to do now than Walt did. He could have been thankful his partner in this mess was a seasoned evader of manhunters.

Tug did not retreat far into the forest. He rode far enough to have cover and he rode southward. His idea was sound: southward was the last direction Felton's men would search. It didn't always work that way but in Tug Carlyle's mind it seemed likely it might work this time. In any case the odds were better.

They worked their way among trees until Tug came to an outcropping with a good easterly view. Where he halted and dismounted there was spiny under-brush, unfit for horse feed but better than a snow bank.

The animals were in need of a respite. They hopped in their hobbles to the nearest thicket and picked carefully in order to avoid thorns.

Tug upended his saddle, leaned against it and looked at Walt Skinner. 'Be dark directly,' he said, and Walt nodded. 'Hopefully when we ride down there they'll figure we're those two fellers from the bear den.'

Walt was a practical man. 'Then what?' he asked.

Tug grinned without warmth. 'Then

we play it by ear. I'd like to get that feller from Brighton an' 'possum belly.'

Walt agreed. 'Hostages.' He studied the man opposite him. 'Are you hungry?'

Tug's tough smile lingered. 'I could eat a skunk right now beginnin' at the butt end if someone would hold its head.'

'What about the woman?'

'If she stays put . . . ' Tug set about building a smoke. Walt watched and said, 'How far does that smell carry?'

Tug nodded, emptied the paper and shifted to get more comfortable.

9

Trading Places

In some ways time is fleet, as with age. In other ways, as with waiting, it crawls. For the fugitives it crawled and that did nothing toward abating their impatience — and hunger.

Dusk passed and that puny moon showed. They rigged out and began angling down out of the forest. There was a light at the Skinner cabin.

Tug was hopeful that most, or at least some of the possemen would have returned to Bridgeport.

Some had but when it was possible to make things out there were still five horses in the corral. Walt was widening the distance between them when Tug growled, 'The house later. Right now it'll be the horses.'

Walt veered back.

They kept the barn between themselves and the house as long as possible. When the light was blocked out they were close enough.

Tug dismounted, started leading his tall horse and Walt followed. He did not ask the question uppermost in his mind. In fact, he didn't make a sound even after it became clear what Tug had in mind.

They made sure there were no horses stalled in the barn before turning toward the corral where several horses stood watching.

Tug went to the gate, freed the big halter snap and Walt roughly brushed him aside, gripped the gate and lifted as he opened it.

The gate dragged, a not uncommon condition; dragging gates made noises.

The animals were warily slow. Tug and his companion stood well aside. The lead horse passed beyond the open gate and put his tail in the air and ran. He was followed by the other horses.

Tug closed the gate, a needless thing

to do unless a person had grown up in the country.

If the freed mounts had all broke past the gate in a thunderous rush . . . but they didn't. Tug winked at Skinner.

They went up through the barn to its front opening and briefly lingered far enough back inside to be unseen from the house.

Darkness helped but two men in the barn did not offset four or five men in the house.

Walt leaned to hiss, 'All right; always set 'em afoot first. Now what?'

Tug was gazing in the direction of the house when he answered.

'Go over there, kick in the door and shoot anyone who moves. Or stay here until someone comes out to pee an' grab him.'

Walt said nothing but he favoured the second suggestion. No one in their right mind would bust into a house when they were outnumbered better than two to one.

Rarely do things happen exactly as

they are supposed to. A man came out of the house but he had Jeff Skinner with him and the man didn't pee, he walked with Walt's son to the chicken house.

Tug murmured, 'Eggs for supper.'

When Jeff came out of the hen house with a hat half full of eggs, the men in the barn clearly heard him address the boy. 'You know where that squatter settlement is?'

'Yes.'

'Would they head for that place?'

'I got no idea.'

'But your pa knows where that place is?'

'He knows. It's a long ride. As far as I know he don't cotton much to homesteaders.'

Jeff closed and latched the hen house door. As he and his guard started toward the house, the man spoke again. 'That other feller, the outlaw.'

'What about him?'

'He patched up your wolf?'

'No. My pa did that. He did that

years back in the army.'

'Which army?'

'There's only one, ain't there?'

'Boy . . . it bothers me. Him a federal lawman takin' up with that outlaw.'

Jeff's reply was fading. The last thing they heard him say was, 'Like I said, he helped me with the wolf. He didn't have to. That was good enough for me'n my pa.'

As the man and boy passed out of hearing distance, Walt said, 'He's like his mother. Decent things mattered more to her than money.'

Tug nodded faintly and leaned in the barn doorway. 'Which one was he?'

Walt had no idea. 'Too dark to tell. We could have grabbed him.'

Tug looked at his companion. 'Jeff didn't sound scairt.'

'He don't scare easy.'

A loud burst of profanity erupted somewhere behind them. Moments later, a thin, wiry shadow appeared in the rear barn opening. The man started up through. He had discovered that he and his companions had been set afoot.

Tug faded into darkness, drew his six-gun and waited before cocking it. The posseman heard and stopped stone still peering ahead.

Tug said, 'Shuck it!'

The thin man dropped his holstered Colt.

Walt stepped close, didn't recognize the man for an excellent reason, he had come north from Brighton. The captive let go an audible sigh, it sounded almost like a groan.

Tug gave an order in a voice that indicated he meant each word. 'Down on the ground. *Get down!*'

The posseman got belly down. As Walt jerked the man's trouser belt free, the man looked up. 'You're as good as caught. They'll be along directly.'

He got no reply as Walt sank to one knee to cinch the belt tightly from in back. As he arose he jerked the posseman up with him. 'How many are in the house?'

The prisoner tested the bindings

behind his back as he answered.

'Ten, an' they'll be comin' out soon.'

Walt sounded sarcastic when he spoke again. 'Not until sun-up, you lyin' bastard.'

'Sooner'n that. They got the woman an' took her back to Felton's jailhouse. She told us where you was goin'. It's a far piece from here but they'll be headin' out in the dark to reach that nest of squatters about sun-up.'

Tug put up his weapon, walked to within two feet of the prisoner and spoke quietly. 'You know different. We're here not over there.'

'Won't make a damn when they find the horses've been run off.' The thin man cocked his head slightly to one side. 'You'll be the one that shot the storekeeper down at Brighton.'

Tug ignored that. 'You're goin' to help us.'

The thin man spat his reply. 'Help you get to Hell, you back-shootin' bastard.'

Tug considered the defiant prisoner

briefly then fired his right fist from the shoulder. Their prisoner dropped in his tracks. Tug was looking down when he said, 'Some rope, Walt, an' some waddin' to stuff in his mouth.'

No one was keeping track of time; when they had gagged and bound the thin man, Tug said, 'Four left.'

Walt said nothing; he had been a manhunter. Manhunters were ordinarily not seasoned in planning, only in hunting those who figured ahead.

He said, 'It'd be nice if they come out one at a time.'

Tug neither agreed nor disagreed. He returned to the front barn opening, saw that all but one lamp was still showing light and spoke over his shoulder.

'Ate and bedded down.'

The prisoner was coming around. He feebly struggled. Neither of his captors looked back.

Tug ruminated out loud. 'Down south they'd set fire an' burn 'em out.' Even a sidelong glance at Walt Skinner in poor light showed his disapproval of that idea as he said, 'It took me'n Jeff two years to make that house, an' if you mean shoot 'em when they run out, partner, that'd be plain murder. We're in enough trouble already.'

Tug inclined his head. 'Another thing we can do that should bring 'em out is fire a few rounds.' He looked at Walt, who nodded his head as he said, 'It'll still be bad odds.' Walt drew his six-gun, stepped barely outside the barn and fired twice in the direction of his log house.

He stepped back and methodically shucked the empty casings and plugged in fresh loads from his shellbelt.

What followed was that someone blew down the mantle of the lamp. Tug swore under his breath. They had accomplished about what happens when someone strikes a wasp nest with a stick.

Tug said, 'Out the back way,' and led off toward the rear barn opening. The nearest protection was the palisaded fence at the hen house. Tug turned in the opposite direction. Walt followed; experienced or not he understood instinctively that his companion was trading space for time.

Tug headed for the nearest stand of trees, but when they halted there he told Skinner unless they were seen or heard he wanted to get around to the back of the house.

Walt required no explanation. He led off utilizing every tree and shadow. They were well along easterly when someone yelled. Whoever he was he had found Tug's thoroughbred and Walt's horse.

To accomplish this at least one of the manhunters had to have covered considerable ground. They both recognized the man who called back: Ames Felton. 'Bring 'em in so's they can't get away.'

The second voice they heard had a slight depth of an echo. This manhunter was furious. Between curses he said, 'They'll be close by,' and got a direct order from the Bridgeport constable.

'Go to the house. Don't let that boy out of your sight!'

Tug followed Skinner on a wide, circuitous route in the direction of the house. The night was still and silent. If it had been daylight their tracks would have been readable.

Where Walt made a sashay to avoid the well-house was not far from the east side of his destination. Tug took the lead toward the southerly, rear of the house.

Commonly the first trees felled to make a house were taken down close by for two reasons, for the house and to provide a clearing.

Clearings under the present circumstance did not favour the fugitives but darkness did.

They made the crossing. Tug halted his momentum with both outstretched hands and struck some steel traps hanging from a spike in the house wall.

Walt turned sharply as Tug cursed under his breath, the sound of rattling traps and their chains was loud enough to be heard as far as the barn.

Silence returned. Tug stopped swearing and led off around the corner of the house.

That posseman who was inside with Jeff would have had to have been deaf not to have heard the noise.

Tug's disgust and anger drove him to move around the corner without looking first. It was a foolish thing to do but there was no one waiting near the rear door.

Walt eased around, went to the door, gripped the latch and lifted. It did not move. The door was barred from the inside.

Walt did not try to force it. He had built this house; he knew how strong that door bar was on the inside. He jerked his head and moved quickly toward the far north-west corner where he halted, sank to one knee and peered around. There was no one in sight and no movement. He arose, faced Tug and quietly said, 'Wish I'd spent the two dollars for a window.'

Tug leaned to watch in the direction of the barn. He saw no one but he and Walt both heard a man try to stifle a cough. The sound came from the west. Whoever was out there was close to being even with the west corner of the house.

A sudden commotion inside erupted when someone struck a piece of furniture. Walt spun back in the direction of the door, stood back and fired three shots at the area of the inside hinge. His last shot, deafening in the night, smashed the hinge. The drawbar fell and Walt kicked the door open.

Someone fired once from the parlour. The slug buried itself in the half-open door. Walt sank to one knee, yelled for his son to lie flat and shot his last three bullets inside.

There was yelling from the yard. It came in different directions where the manhunters had fanned out in their search.

Tug bumped Walt out of the way and got inside the house. When muzzle blast showed he fired chest high above it and heard the gun fall, followed by the fall of the gunman.

Being inside had an advantage but the odds were still respectable. Even with the departure of the rangemen in the bear den they were overwhelming — except for the log walls of the Skinner cabin.

This had not gone the way Tug would have preferred, but Walt's interpretation of someone being struck and overturning a chair in the process had taken whatever initiative Tug had.

Walt's boy was in a dark corner with his wolf. She growled otherwise the boy's position might not have been easily found.

Walt went over there. Tug moved toward the front without paying attention to the voices behind him. He nearly fell over a man on the floor. He paused long enough to find the gun and shove it into his waistband.

The yelling had stopped. Again the silence was settled and remained.

The odour of burnt gunpowder was noticeable as Tug considered cracking the door a fraction. What deterred him was the sound of leather scraping over wood. Someone was too close. Walt may have worried about being unable to afford a glass window but Tug didn't.

Whoever was out there, and most likely it was more than one man, the log walls were between those inside and those outside.

A gravelly voice called. Tug recognized the voice of Constable Felton.

'We're goin' to burn you bastards out!'

Tug did not return the call, Walt did. 'Try it! Felton, what'd you do with the woman?'

Felton's tone softened. 'We got her out here . . . Marshal? I'll make you a trade: you fellers come out an' she can go free.'

Tug snorted and interrupted the exchange. 'You lyin' bastard. She's locked up in town.'

This time Felton hung fire before

calling again. 'Carlyle? We're goin' to hang you from the sour apple tree!'

Someone, possibly the Bridgeport lawman, fired off a round that struck the front log wall with an unmistakable sound. Someone out in the night had a rifle instead of a carbine.

Jeff came forward, stepped over the dead man and spoke to his father. 'I'll get up into the loft.'

Walt turned. 'Stay here.'

'Pa, they can't see me up there. I can open the outside door a crack.'

Walt slapped his son lightly on the shoulder and walked swiftly toward the back of the house where a knotted rope hung overhead. He pulled it and the loft ladder came down. He started up it as his son spoke to Tug. 'It was my idea.'

Tug was straining to hear noise from the outside. 'Stay here,' he growled and Jeff went to the dark side of the room with a shotgun. There were loopholes over there but none large enough to accommodate a gun with two barrels.

Tug pressed close; he wasn't sure but he thought he had caught the sound of shod horses.

Not until the sound was strong enough to be identified with certainty did Tug's heart begin to sink. They had caught their horses and Felton would certainly send to Bridgeport for armed reinforcements.

A solitary gunshot sounded from the loft door. To the east, a man yelped. The loft-shot brought a fusillade of gunfire — into the logs below. If Walt's muzzle blast had been seen, the possemen must have thought it came from lower down. It was dark enough for that mistake to be made.

Someone was swearing in a loud, disgusted voice that made it impossible to discern those shod-horse sounds. At the time, Tug couldn't have cared less. If he'd thought about it at all it would have been to estimate the time it would take for a mounted man to reach Bridgeport, round up more men and return.

His guess was that it couldn't be accomplished before sunrise and because Tug Carlyle, like many others, did not own a watch he had no idea how long that would be.

What he *did* understand was that a siege behind log walls of two men and a boy against daunting odds could not last long once daylight arrived.

10

Embarrassed Lawmen

When another lull arrived, Tug ignored Felton's comment about having Beth Holden with him. He and Walt had bought off two men, another one was dead on the floor behind him; he had been recognized by both fugitives; the thin man they had caught at the barn.

The problem with arriving at an accurate count was based on Tug's lack of knowledge of exactly how many possemen were out there.

The three from Brighton, Felton and possibly another two or three. Add to those odds the number of others who might arrive about daybreak . . . Tug leathered his six-gun, rolled and lighted a smoke and shook his head; by now they were in enemy country. *Son of a bitch!*

His attention was attracted by a loud whistle, the kind men made using two fingers. Walt came down from the loft. 'They're going to hit us hard.'

Tug did not comment. Again, he heard shod horses, this time the sound was unmistakable.

'Reinforcements,' Walt exclaimed, and Tug shook his head. 'Not from Bridgeport; they haven't had time to get there and back.'

That loud whistle sounded for the second time and was followed by a profane exclamation. Jeff came from his dark place and addressed his father. 'Good thing we put off the chinking until fall.' The older man heeded the boy but with no interest. That whistler cut loose again.

Jeff spoke again. 'There's horsemen up yonder.'

This time his father turned. 'Where?'

The boy gestured. 'Up yonder. I couldn't see 'em real well from the place between the logs where that chinkin' had fallen out. Hard to make 'em out it bein' dark an' them stayin' back in the trees.'

There was another shouted interruption from the yard. This time it didn't sound like Ames Felton, the voice was clearer, the words sharp. 'Carlyle! Come out an' we'll take you back to Brighton . . . no lynchin'. All right?'

Tug had no chance to reply. A deep, strong voice called loudly. Walt stiffened at the sound of the voice; it was slightly accented.

'You in the barn. Come out, no guns, hands atop your heads!'

Walt made an almost breathless sound. 'Carl Freiberg!'

Tug leaned against the wall. 'You sure? How'd he know?'

'I'm sure. I'd know the way he talks in a crowd.'

Walt went to the door but did not open it. The strong accented voice spoke again. 'Come *oudt*. We'll burn the barn down. You *godt* one minute . . . You want to fight? Good. There's twelve of us. Let's fight.'

For a long moment there wasn't a sound until someone on the east side of the house accidentally kicked a pile of kindling wood, an inadvertent accident, darkness made footing uncertain even if stalkers watched where they walked.

Tug went to the kitchen wall, rapped on it with his gun barrel and spoke loudly enough for the stumbler to hear. 'Go around front. Get with your friends, leave your gun where you're standin'.'

There was no reply, nor was there any way to know what the stalker would do.

Constable Felton's gravelly voice called loudly. 'Are you from that squatter settlement? This isn't none of your business. Go on back where you belong.'

This time the answer was a gunshot loud enough to indicate it hadn't come from a saddle gun. As a rule, homesteaders preferred rifles. The impact of a slug striking near the rear opening at the barn wasn't audible to the men in the house but possemen anywhere near the barn heard it.

There was another lull. Tug doused his smoke and gazed at the Skinners. 'Big palaver in the barn,' he said dryly, put his gaze squarely on Walt. 'You told 'em over yonder the law was after us? I expect Gretchen figured when they learned Jeff left he'd head for home then we would too.'

Tug considered the boy, and smiled without speaking. Someday he might have a son.

Another rifle blast broke the heightened stillness and Ames Felton called out, 'We'll talk. You fellers ride down into the yard.'

The accented answer was brusque. 'You come *oudt* of the barn. You come where we can see you. No guns, just walk out and we'll talk.'

There was another of those long silences. Tug guessed Felton was having trouble with the men from Brighton, especially their leader, the Brighton lawman.

Felton finally agreed. 'I'll come out. You fellers ride on down.'

Evidently the large man with the accent was no novice. His answer was: 'You *all* come *oudt*. Come out without guns. Make up your mind. It's getting cold.'

This time the lull was not as long. Walt cracked the door. He jerked his head. Tug went over. Visibility was poor but silhouetted movement showed three men leaving the barn. They walked out where they would be visible and stopped while the Bridgeport constable cupped both hands and called out.

'No guns. Let's talk.'

Walt said, 'Lyin' bastard! There's more'n three.'

Tug ageed without saying so as he watched several mounted men sift through the timber at wide intervals.

There wasn't much he could have done without going outside to call a warning. He was moving in the direction of the door when one of those long-guns was fired north of where the emerging homesteaders were visible. Jeff, back at his spy hole crack between wall logs said, 'At the barn. There was one of them homesteaders back there.'

Tug wagged his head and addressed Walt. 'Your squatter friend's no greenhorn. He sent someone down on foot to the rear of the barn . . . Was he ever a soldier?'

Walt had no time to answer. Two homesteaders cut across northward toward the rear of the barn. Watery moonlight reflected off rifle barrels.

The large man with the bass voice called to the three waiting besiegers. 'That one you left in the barn, if he's got friends with him we'll hang them all.'

Among the three exposed besiegers there was not a sound as the large man on his 1,200-pound combination horse cleared the last of the trees. He had a rifle across the saddle swell. Because he was riding eastward Tug could not tell whether he also had a six-gun on the right side.

That forceful constable from Brighton, Frank Kellogg, waited until the big man on the big horse stopped, then said, 'Mister, you're interferin' with the course of the law. If you got any sense you'll turn around and — '

The big man's deep voice interrupted with a growl. 'What law? You make it up as you go along? If you got a hide-out gun after you been told to leave the guns back yonder, we'll hang you first.'

One of Kellogg's Brighton possemen gave the constable a sharp elbow.

The big homesteader looked toward the house. 'Anyone hurt in there?'

Walt yanked the door wide and answered. 'No one's hurt.'

There were four men on big farm horses behind the big man. Each one had a rifle instead of the customary carbine. They sat their horses like stone carvings.

Two men came around from behind the barn herding two other men whose hands were clasped atop their hats. Frank Kellogg showed his temperament when he addressed the larger home-steader. 'You're buttin' in where you got no business an' — '

'Shut up! Who are you?'

'Constable Frank Kellogg from down at Brighton. That feller in the house with Skinner robbed my town some days back, an' shot our storekeeper. Mister, you know what an accessory is?'

The big man neither moved nor spoke.

Kellogg continued, 'I didn't expect you would, bein' one of them squatters an' a foreigner.'

Carl Freiberg held out his rifle for one of his companions to take it, dismounted and started walking. Felton squawked and moved to intervene. Freiberg brushed him aside with one hand, stopped in front of Kellogg and growled, 'You talk tough. Let's see how tough you are.'

Frank Kellogg was an overbearing, disagreeable individual but he was no fool. The man facing him was easily fifty or sixty pounds heavier and about four or five inches taller. Even in poor light he appeared to be solid and powerful. Farming made men like that.

Kellogg said, 'Wait a minute. You strike an officer of the law an' you'll be in trouble up to your — '

When the blow landed it sounded like someone broke a piece of wood over his knee. Kellogg went backwards, sidewards and down. One of his posse riders grinned.

Ames Felton said, 'What's your name, squatter?'

Freiberg picked Felton off the ground and hurled him against his possemen. Two of them went down. The third man sidestepped in time.

He faced in the direction of the house. 'Walt . . . ?'

Skinner came out followed by Tug and Jeff. Freiberg looked pleased. 'What you told Gretchen. Well, what are friends for! Do you want to hang these men?'

Walt shook his head and Tug spoke from behind him. 'Let 'em shed their britches, their underdrawers'n boots an' walk back where they come from.'

Freiberg remained expressionless for a moment, then smiled and nodded. He faced the possemen. 'Do it!'

They obeyed in stony silence. Being naked from the waist down was bad enough even on a dark night and if they got back to Bridgeport before sun-up, covering that distance barefoot . . . One of them looked at Carl Freiberg. 'There's two more fellers off in the trees somewhere.'

Tug shook his head. 'They left the country,' he said and added nothing more.

Walt sent his son to look after Mary Todd. Off in the east there was a knife-blade streak of light. The half-naked possemen would never reach their settlement in time.

Tug walked up to Ames Felton. 'Where is she, you son of bitch? S'help me Gawd I'll hang you myself. *Where is she!*'

'I sent her back to be locked up.'

'You said she was here.'

'Well . . . I had an idea since she freed you fellers one of you was sweet on her . . . '

Tug was shoved aside and Walt took his place. Walt didn't say a word, he struck the Bridgeport lawman in the soft parts, hard. Felton's breath rushed out. Walt forced him to stand and hit him three times, twice in the face where his son had been hit and the last time in the centre of the chest. Felton went down in a sprawling heap.

Freiberg watched stoically. When Felton collapsed, he asked Walt what he had done and Walt answered crisply.

'He beat up on Jeff.'

Freiberg considered the unconscious fat man and spoke in an imperturbable way. 'Let's hang him.'

Tug was beginning to wonder if homesteaders resolved their differences with hang ropes when two men from the settlement dragged a dead man out of the house. In slightly better light Tug recognized him as the thin man he and

Walt had left trussed in the barn.

No one paid particular attention.
Their attention was diverted when Tug
approached Felton and said, 'How
much did you take out of my
saddle-bags?'

No one had any idea that this would
be a good time to play hide and seek,
including the Bridgeport lawman. 'Two
hundred dollars. The saddle-bags're in
the barn.'

Felton's companions looked at him.
They had seen a pair of saddle-bags
earlier at the jailhouse but had attached
little importance to them; many horsemen carried either saddle-bags or
saddle pockets, but the longer they
stood looking at Felton an eventual
thought soaked in.

One man said, 'Why'd you fetch
them bags along, Ames?'

The constable fidgeted slightly and
before he could answer the same
questioner said, 'Ames, you figured to
keep the money?'

Felton ignored the accuser and Frank

Kellogg was clawing the ground to hoist himself up onto all fours. He leaned to fully arise and Tug moved to lend a hand. He waited until Kellogg was on his feet then turned back to Ames Felton to ask what Felton figured to do with that money and this time it was the Brighton constable who spoke. He was not quite steady on his feet but that didn't affect his voice.

'Ames, you thievin' bastard.'

Felton started to talk when that posse rider who had ridden with him said, 'Ames, you double-crossin', lyin' son of a bitch!'

Carl Freiberg growled for the posse-man to take his hand away from his holster.

Big-bored rifles pointing at the posseman were a powerful inducement to obey; the hand moved clear.

Faintly discernible shadows moved from the barn in the direction of the congregated men. They were Freiberg's friends who had passed through the barn after a cursory search.

One of them was familiar to Walt Skinner and Carl Freiberg but to none of the others. This man spoke to Freiberg in a guttural language the others did not understand and he faced Walt. 'There's some loose horses outside the corral.'

Walt's response was practical. 'Let 'em in. They'll belong to these fellers.'

'There's a big thoroughbred with 'em, Carl.'

Tug said, 'Let him in too. He belongs to me.'

The homesteaders went back to the barn area and Frank Kellogg, fully recovered except for soreness, addressed Carl Freiberg.

'Those two are wanted down at Brighton. One killed the storekeeper. Shot him in the back as he was escaping.'

For Freiberg and his companions who had rescued the forted-up men, this was a shock. They had thought they were riding to the rescue.

The large man faced Walt. 'It's the truth?'

Walt couldn't answer. He faced Tug with raised eyebrows.

Tug gave the only answer he knew. 'Far as I know I didn't hit anyone . . . an' if this gent was shot in the back . . . I was ridin' north as hard as I could. I fired back. For as far as I could see no one went down.' Walt looked at Kellogg who returned the look with a baleful one.

'You shot your gun empty,' Kellogg exclaimed. 'There was men shootin' back.'

Tug interrupted. 'I was ridin' hard northward. I shot back from northward. How in hell could I have shot someone who was facing me, in the back, which would be southward?'

Kellogg did not relent. 'We'll find that out when I get you down to Brighton.'

Freiberg growled again. 'I don't think you take nobody down to Brighton. Constable Felton's the law up here, you ain't.' The large homesteader faced Walt Skinner. 'You come back with us. If they want war we'll give them one. We've been fighting cowmen for ten years, we can fight some more.'

A raw-boned, shockle-headed homesteader spat aside and addressed Tug. 'Why do they want you? You shot a man in Brighton?'

Kellogg answered curtly. 'For robbin' the bank an' the general store down in Brighton!'

If that statement was meant to intimidate the tobacco-chewing homesteader, it didn't. He said, 'Right or wrong, you don't come to this country and arrest no one.'

Carl Freiberg had been studying Tug Carlyle. He said, 'You didn't shoot no one down there?'

Tug shook his head. 'It was a running fight. I didn't see anyone go down.'

'But you robbed those places?'

'Yes.'

Freiberg surprised them all when he smiled and spoke again. 'You come with us. Walt? He is a friend of yours?'

Skinner didn't hesitate. 'Yes. I'll tell you on the way, Carl.'

Freiberg looked at the trouserless possemen. 'Start walking,' he said and told his companions to bring up their horses.

One man spoke agitatedly. 'Mister . . . our pants?'

Freiberg shook his head. 'Not even your boots.'

Frank Kellogg snarled, 'I'll have the army after you. You've just taken prisoners that belong to the law an' defied two lawmen.'

Freiberg considered the bruised speaker. 'Do that,' he said and repeated what he'd told his companions. 'Bring up the horses.'

11

Waiting

When the yard was empty of pedestrian posse riders and their leaders, Jeff came from the house to tell his father he would stay with Mary Todd. She needed him.

Walt's brow creased. Before he could speak the big homesteader said, 'Who is Mary Todd?'

Jeff explained. Freiberg stood briefly in thought then addressed Jeff's father. 'Do you know how to make a horse sling?'

Walt shook his head.

Freiberg spoke aside to the rawboned man with the cud in his cheek. 'Find canvas. We make a sling. That's how we moved wounded men in Germany during the wars.'

Tug remained silent, but he would

have bet his thoroughbred the wolf wouldn't go along peacefully.

There was budding daylight by the time the horsemen — with Mary Todd in her two-horse-sling — left the yard on their way to the uplands, through the forest toward the homesteader settlement.

Mary Todd fought right up until Jeff climbed into the sling with her. After that when jolting caused pain she only occasionally whimpered.

The pair of men riding the horses with the sling between them kept their mounts moving in unison. For the wolf it couldn't have been comfortable even when the route was not difficult. One of the horsemen laughed and his companion grinned as he said, 'No one's ever goin' to believe this. I hate wolves. They kill calves.'

The laughing man spoke too soon. Even with Jeff in the sling with the wolf and despite the difficulty of managing its splinted leg Mary Todd wanted to jump out.

It was a long ride. They didn't see rooftops until the sun was well up. Walt asked Freiberg what his daughter had told him and the large, stoic man smiled without speaking. Some men, in fact many men, were averse to repeating private conversations even to friends. Carl Freiberg acted as though he hadn't heard.

He said Ames Felton was a poor excuse for a human being and enlarged to the extent of telling Walt things he did not know. One of them was Felton's trip to the settlement last year when he asked his daughter to go walking in the evening and this time the large man did not smile. 'That man Felton tried to separate us. I told him to get on his horse and not to come near us again.'

Tug, who was riding behind did not say what he was thinking: Felton would be back. This time with the army if he could get it to do it, if not then with another posse, this time a large one.

He worried about Beth Holden. He particularly didn't like the idea of her

197

being at the mercy of Felton.

That rawboned, outspoken home-steader rode up beside Tug when the trees began to thin out and said, 'I got a cousin who has a shop down in Brighton. In fact it was him writin' me how wonderful this country was that got me to come out here. He'd likely know about that storekeeper gettin' shot. Like you said, bullets don't go around corners.'

There were lights at the settlement, some brighter than others. Not every-one could afford coal oil for lamps and used candles.

By the time they were easing down from the uplands the lights had been extinguished.

Tug had a little of the disapproval of homesteaders that was endemic throughout the cattle rural west, but not having been involved with cattle for some years his disapproval was minimal, it helped that he had been treated well on his earlier visit to this place.

Two squatters loped ahead. One held his rifle aloft and wigwagged with it. He was younger than his companion, an older man not much given to celebratory gestures. People were waiting; mothers and wives in particular.

Freiberg led to his corral and handed down his rifle to an older woman before dismounting. They embraced. She clung longer than he did before scurrying away.

Walt looped his reins, went where a sturdy blonde girl was standing and held out both hands. She took them. Under the eyes of Gretchen's father that was all they dared do but Tug could see the look on the girl's face.

Getting Mary Todd out of her sling required three strong men. She was not accustomed to being lifted.

Two women watched Jeff pet and talk to his wolf. It was as close as either of them had ever been to a wolf; homesteaders had reason to fear wolves and crippled or not Mary Todd could not be mistaken for anything but what she was.

The animals were cared for and fed. Most of the squatters faded among the houses. Carl Freiberg took both fugitives, Jeff and even the lame wolf to his large, comfortable log house where a sturdy woman — a spitting image of Gretchen — jerked her head at her daughter and they both disappeared into the kitchen.

Carl Freiberg lighted a pipe that had a small tassel at the mouthpiece, brought forth a bottle of whiskey, poured three small glasses full, handed them to Tug and Walt with a toast neither of them understood but raised their glasses nonetheless.

Freiberg asked Tug about the killing down in Brighton. Tug explained what was a fact, a man riding hard northward couldn't shoot a man who was facing him northward in the back which was southward.

The large man digested that without comment, went to stand near the fire and removed the pipe to address Walt Skinner.

'They will come here,' Freiberg said. 'We will be ready.'

Walt dropped into a chair, and shook his head, watched his son feeding Mary Todd and said, 'It's not your fight, Carl. We'll saddle up and head out after breakfast.'

The big man turned to knock dottle into the fire, turned back and said, 'No. You stay. If you go they will arrest us for helping you.'

Tug sighed. He not only hadn't shot anyone; he shouldn't have wasted time helping the boy with his wolf and its broken leg. He looked at Walt, sitting tiredly, and said, 'I'll head out. Somehow this didn't come out right. By now I should've been fifty miles on my way.'

'To where?' Walt asked and Tug shrugged.

'To anywhere as long as it's a fair distance from here.'

The big homesteader spoke again in

his almost guttural voice. 'If you didn't kill anybody . . . '

'I robbed their town.'

Freiberg made the gesture of someone brushing something aside. 'Some other place I wouldn't like it. In Brighton they treat homesteaders like dirt. Mister, you stay.'

They were summoned from the kitchen. As Tug ate he estimated time. If the lawmen got back to Brighton before noon and got back a-horseback with more men . . . he dove into the breakfast. Felton and the disagreeable lawman from Brighton couldn't reach the homesteader settlement until midnight or later.

Gretchen's mother shooed her out of the kitchen. She and Walt left the house with a hot sun climbing. Gretchen's mother said something in an ugly language to her husband and he nodded.

Tug went to look in on his horse, sat in newday warmth against a fragrant hay shock and fell asleep.

When he awakened someone was exploring his ear with a beardless barley stalk.

It wasn't Jeff it was his father. He sat on the ground too. 'Carl went among the squatters. They're worked up to fight. They got reason. They been burnt out, beat up, some been lynched. I guess folks can be driven to places like this by abuse.'

Tug nodded. 'Folks reach a limit. Thing is, Walt, this whole damned mess is my fault. Gettin' you dragged in, gettin' these farmers ready to fight.' Tug paused. 'You take care of that boy. A youngster that's got a feelin' for them as need help'll make a good man.'

Tug shoved out his hand. Walt shook and watched Tug walk away. He was still sitting there in shade with hay-fragrance when Gretchen appeared. She smiled. 'Two men rode up yonder to keep watch.' She sat down beside Skinner. 'There will be trouble. My father said it was bound to come. Those people over the hills don't like homesteaders. He said it was a matter of time before they came here.'

Walt watched Tug out of sight before speaking. 'There goes a good man,' he said, and the girl followed her companion's line of sight.

'Is he leaving? He's an outlaw.'

Walt turned his head. How does one explain some things? He said nothing.

Gretchen changed the subject. 'Jeff's wolf's taken to my mother. She feeds her scraps. Ma's always been afraid of wolves.'

Walt grinned. 'Mary Todd's been with us long enough so sometimes it seems she's not a wolf. When she can travel she'll leave an' Jeff'll learn another lesson.'

'Maybe she'll come back, Walt.'

He shrugged. 'Maybe. Folks can tame wild animals but they're still wild. Gretchen . . . ?'

'Yes.'

'How old do your folks think people should get married?'

She reddened without lowering her

eyes. 'When they're ready.'

Walt had the next question formed to ask but a rider coming down the hill slope behind them interrupted. He was doing something reckless. No one in their right mind loped a horse down a steep slope unless he had good reason.

Walt got to his feet, dusted off and watched the rider head for the Freiberg place. Gretchen softly but urgently said, 'I'd better go home. Walt?'

'Yes'm.'

Her colour remained high when she said, 'When they're ready,' and hurried in the direction of home.

Gretchen's father and the rider talked while the horseman remained in the saddle. Walt would have had to have been much closer to hear but clearly the conversation, short as it was, inspired both the rider and Freiberg to take action.

Walt followed Gretchen until he was face to face with her father. The big older man said, 'They're coming, eleven of them. They'll be here late tonight or in the morning.'

Looking past, Walt saw Tug Carlyle watching the sudden activity. He started slowly walking back.

The messenger rode through the settlement passing his message; shortly afterwards men appeared with rifles. Walt and Tug met out near the Freiberg corral where Tug said, 'I'd better stay since this is all my fault.'

Walt said nothing. That agitated messenger was going back up the hill on a fresh horse. Tug shook his head. Whoever fired first would get the blame later.

He turned to Walt. 'Someone'd better ride up there an' make sure some hothead don't start a war. All that would be needed is for one of these folks to fire first an' kill a posseman an' the army'll come.'

Walt walked briskly to the Freiberg place, met Gretchen's father walking towards a shed carrying a milking bucket. He repeated what Tug had said and Freiberg nodded. He had already sent two older settlers up to find the watchers and keep them in check.

He considered Walt unsmilingly. Freiberg was not without sensibilities, but he belonged to a race of people who did not commonly show feeling in their expression. He said, 'You'n my girl . . . '

'When this mess is finished, Carl.'

The older man nodded. 'We talked about it. Gretchen's mother an' me. She saw it coming a long time ago.' Freiberg put down the bucket and extended a ham-sized hand. 'We got no objections,' he said. They shook and the older man resumed his march to the milking shed with the bucket in one hand.

Walt saw Gretchen's silhouette in shadows near the house. Before he could move the girl entered the house and closed the door.

There was activity among the settlers. Evidently they, like Carl Freiberg, had expected something like this from the men over the mountain.

The older woman who had first

welcomed Tug came and asked how many were coming. Walt referred her to Gretchen's father. When Walt appeared and Tug asked the same question Walt's answer was circuitous. 'I don't know but it'll be as many as they figure they'd need.'

A wisp of a youngish man came up. If Tug had seen him before he couldn't remember. The thin man said, 'By rights they can't do this.'

Tug gazed at the slight individual as Walt said, 'This here is Roger Herman. Roger, this here is — '

'I know who he is: Tug. Everyone knows. What I was sayin' is that they can't use soldiers.'

Walt's reply was short. 'As far as I know, Roger, no one's said they're bringin' the army.'

As though Walt hadn't spoken the wispy individual pronounced his conviction. 'Before a state is incorporated into the Union it's governed as a territory and territories are policed by the army. When a state joins the Union enforcement is the job of civilian lawmen.'

Walt nodded acceptance and as the slight man walked away, Walt explained. 'He's a fee lawyer by trade. Back East. He homesteaded; damned if I know why. He don't know one end of a plough from the other end.'

Tug looked after the fee lawyer who was heading for the Freiberg house. There were misfits wherever folks congregated.

The older settlers went up the hill on 1,000-pound horses with rifle butts balanced on upper legs. Tug watched without saying what he was thinking: farmers on horseback!

The elderly soul who had initially fed Tug and Walt went briskly in the direction of the settlement store. She nodded without changing leads in her stride.

Tug privately speculated about the war-making capability of homesteaders and as though Walt had read his mind Walt said, 'Half of 'em fought in the

War Between the States. Carl, well, that's why he emigrated. He was picked up and forced into two German armies. They're not as helpless as a man might think.'

Tug was only slightly reassured. He went out to visit his horse and got a surprise, several bands of riflemen were astride but the horses were clearly heading for the settlement. Some nodded in his direction but most didn't. He wondered aloud to the thoroughbred how news carried fast enough to reach outlying farms. Coincidence? Not a chance; farmers didn't ride around carrying the cumbersome long-barrelled guns.

When he walked back dusk was settling. There were lights in every residence and about the time he reached the wide, dusty roadway a horse fight broke out on the west side of town. It ended swiftly when some knowledgeable resident threw a bucket of water.

There was smoke arising from almost

every kitchen stove or fireplace. Tug found a hewn step outside a darkened shop and sat on it.

Jeff Skinner appeared out of shadows, smiled and said, 'Mary Todd's gettin' so's she puts a little weight on the broken leg.'

It was a pleasant diversion for Tug's dark mood; if there was a war it would be his fault.

He said, 'I want you to do somethin' for me. Stay with your wolf. No matter what happens outside, boy, stay inside with her.'

Tug should have anticipated the boy's reaction. 'I can't do that, Mr Carlyle. If Pa's in it I'll be in it with him. Do you expect there'll be a scrap?'

Tug considered the youth as he dryly said, 'It's got all the reason for one.'

Jeff answered characteristically for someone who was friendly with farmers. 'They got reason. Pa says you can push folks just so far then they get their backs up.'

Tug nodded absently. The boy's

answer hadn't surprised him. Jeff had stood up to the possemen over yonder; he'd do the same over here.

What he said next did not surprise Tug either. 'They're gettin' ready. If they ride down into the settlement they'll get a surprise.'

Tug had no difficulty believing that. Those armed men from beyond the settlement on their oversized horses would add to the numbers and while Tug had no idea what the total would be, he would have bet new money it was more than eleven.

After Jeff departed, an older man, big, rawboned, dressed as though he'd just come from the field came along wearing a holstered belt-gun and a shell-belt. He paused to expectorate, looked at Tug and spoke bluntly in a gravelly voice. 'My name's Lefler. James Lefler. I run a few head an' farm out a ways. You'd be that outlaw feller come with Walt Skinner. Right?'

Tug nodded. The rough-looking individual gave a fair idea of his personality. He called a spade a spade.

Tug said, 'Does that thing shoot, Mr Lefler?'

The old man shifted his cud before replying. 'Friend, that gun was taken off a Union officer at Sharp's Ferry. It'll shoot. Someone said it'll be the constable from Bridgeport with a dozen or so possemen. He'll need two, three times that many.'

Tug was tired. He smiled up at the farmer. 'I hope you're right, friend. If they're out-numbered maybe they'll talk.'

James Lefler's reply was a clear indication he hoped there would be no talk. 'Every time I've rode over there them townsfolk wrinkled their nose at me. Acted like they was doin' a favour to sell me supplies. Mister, there's no excuse for bad manners. You agree?'

Tug agreed.

Lefler walked northward, paused to jettison another expectoration and faded in the late dusk.

Tug stretched out his legs and leaned

back. If he rode up yonder and surrendered to the possemen . . . Naw; that wouldn't stop them. Not now, not after they'd been roughed up and humiliated. They'd want blood.

He rolled and lit a smoke. It was a beautiful evening. The kind made for lovers to stroll; the kind folks sat by a fire and read books or visited.

Restlessness set in. Tug left his seat and walked as far as the most distant settlement buildings, turned and walked back.

There was activity and lights at the Freibergs' place. Plans were being finalized; the squatters were organizing to redress years of wrongs and abuse. That kind of mood left no doubt that someone was going to go back tied belly-down across saddles, and home-steader women would be crying.

Someone trilled a sharp whistling sound from the overhead timber. Tug had no idea what that meant; surely the possemen would not attack after nightfall. Even Indians knew better than to do that, although their reasons were different; warriors killed at night were destined to spend eternity wandering in darkness.

Tug met the old woman who had first befriended him. She was scuttling from the direction of a brightly lighted log house. At sight of Tug she said, 'They're goin' to get burnt. We ain't as helpless as they think squatters are.'

Tug nodded and went as far as the Freiberg place; men were in the yard as well as inside the house. There were lights showing from every room.

He didn't own a watch nor would it have made any difference if he'd had one. Plans were being perfected. He'd never been in a war but what he saw — and felt — throughout the settlement inclined him to suspect this was how wars were planned — and fought.

12

By Stealth

Being tired was not the same as being sleepy although under some circumstances there was a comparison. Tug had been tired most of the late day but it was impossible to think in terms of sleep. He was in a place where lights rarely burned after supper-time and it seemed that every light, lamps and candles, were showing with wide gaps between.

His impression of the settlement had been favourable after his first view of it. There were shade trees, sturdily built houses, mostly of logs, a few made from rough slab wood. Fragrant smoke arose from a place that clearly had been settled by people seeking what natives took for granted: security and privacy.

Tug Carlyle had for the last few years

thought of settling down. His occupation had taken him over considerable territory. This place had the makings of something that would endure after the animosity died.

A quiet voice interrupted his reverie. 'Mister Carlyle?'

He turned to face Gretchen Freiberg. 'Evening, ma'am.' She accepted that and moved past common civilities.

'Were you in the war?' she asked.

'No. Too young.'

'My pa was; in several wars.'

Tug had no difficulty believing that. He asked a blunt question. 'You'n Walt . . . ?'

It was too dark to see colour mount in her face. 'Were you ever married, Mr Carlyle?'

'No ma'am; in my line of work there's no time for it . . . I'd take it kindly if you called me Tug.'

She accepted that without saying it for the moment.

'Walt asked me to marry him.'

'Congratulations. Walt's a good man.'

She became busy with a tiny handkerchief which she twisted as she spoke. 'He wants you to stay.'

That didn't surprise Tug regardless of the impossibility of it. 'It'd be easy to stay, ma'am, but not practical for me.'

'If you gave them back their money?'

That was not easy to answer. He cleared his throat and concentrated on the nearest lighted house. That money was going to set him up. She surprised him with what she said next. 'You didn't shoot that storekeeper in Brighton. Pa was there. He can put a name to the man who did kill him. He was in Brighton when you robbed down there. He was at the smithy. The man who shot the storekeeper is a person named Mitchell; he does odd jobs around Brighton. Pa saw him aim at the storekeeper's back from down at the blacksmith's place.'

'Your pa never mentioned this, ma'am. Not around me anyway.'

'My name's Gretchen, not ma'am. He never told anyone until this evening when he told my mother an' some men in our parlour. Pa holds things back. That's his way. My mother was shocked. So were the men in the parlour. Pa said before the fight starts he wants to talk to the posse leaders.'

Tug pondered. Even if her father had told the truth down in Brighton it would have been his word in a place where homesteaders were disliked.

He asked if Walt had been present when her father had related what he had seen down yonder.

She shook her head. 'Walt was with me out back by the cow shed. When I got back my mother told me.'

Tug's thoughts held his total attention. Whatever Gretchen Freiberg might have said he would have missed entirely.

'Ma'am, do me a favour. Go find Walt an' tell him to meet me at the corral. Will you do that?'

'Yes. When? Right now?'

'Yes'm. Right now.'

It was a long wait. Walt was up to his

ears helping plan the course of action when dawn arrived. The wait gave Tug ample time to think. When Walt appeared, Tug said, 'You got somethin' against stolen money?'

It was a question requiring thought. Walt nodded. 'Why?'

'You're goin' to have to send Jeff off to school directly, and after this set-to you might want to go somewhere else an' settle. Those things'll cost money, Walt — '

'Hold it, Tug! That's not your money to give. Jeff an' I'll make out. We did fine when we come here; we'll do that same somewhere else if we got to.'

Tug nodded. That was about the answer he had expected. He shoved out a hand. 'I'll be movin' along. Sorry I got you'n the lad into such a mess.'

Walt slowly shook his head. 'You stay. It would have come to a head without you. The bad feeling's been around since these folk took up land cowmen been usin' for years. They'll play hell whether you're here or not. You're just an excuse.'

Tug leaned on the corral stringers. 'I'll ride out an' give myself up. They'll head back with their prisoner.'

Walt scowled. 'You don't get it through your head. They're comin' here to settle the score about squatters. You just happen to give 'em an excuse. Tug, if it comes to a fight they'll need every man. You don't owe me a thing. You can go but these people . . . '

'All right. I'll stay.'

Walt relaxed. Farmers on horseback or on foot were rarely a fair match against cowmen. Walt was convinced there was going to be a war. Walt had to get back to the Freiberg place. Earlier he'd been surprised at what he had learned from Gretchen's father.

Tug waited a bit then also went in the direction of the Freiberg house, but he entered by the back door which opened into the kitchen where a fine iron stove with elegant curlicues was alternately sending forth popping sounds and waves of heat.

Jeff was kneeling with Mary Todd. He looked up from an expressionless face, watched Tug close the rear door and returned his attention to his bitch wolf. Mary Todd thumped the floorboards several times with her tail.

Talking men in the parlour did not always say distinguishable words but Tug caught enough to recognize a council of war.

He sank to one knee beside Jeff and absently stroked the wolf. She had been stroked so much lately she took it as her due.

Jeff said, 'Did you ever soldier, Mr Carlyle?'

'No. Never did.'

'He sure did. I never heard Gretchen say her pa'd been a soldier overseas where they come from.'

Tug leaned to listen but the palaver was finished. He heard men leaving the house and, as he stood up, Gretchen's mother came into the kitchen carrying a tray of cups. She did not act surprised. She said, 'I'll make you something to eat. You sit down.'

Tug sat on a chair on the far side of a large table. Gretchen's father came into the kitchen and stopped stone still at sight of Tug before giving a short nod and going where Jeff was scratching the wolf's back. He smiled as he said, 'You'll never get rid of that wolf, boy. She's spoilt.'

Carl Freiberg turned to face Tug. 'You will stay?'

Tug nodded and leaned back as Gretchen's mother placed a platter of hot food in front of him.

Her husband sat opposite Tug without speaking for a long moment. 'I wish there was more than eleven,' he said, and did not explain but spoke on another topic.

'I saw the storekeeper killed in Brighton. I was down at the smithy. I saw Cal Mitchell shoot him in the back. That's why I believed you when you said you didn't see how you could shoot anyone, or we wouldn't have brought you back with us.'

There were two responses, both questions. Tug chose neither when he spoke. 'They can have the money. To me there's no sense to gettin' some of you settler folk killed over somethin' you had no hand in.'

The large man eased back in his chair looking steadily at Tug. 'They want the money, sure, but what they want most is to burn us out so's we'll leave the country.'

Tug nodded. He'd heard something like this before. 'You'll outnumber 'em mister, but these are men who been using guns since they was children.'

Gretchen's father's eyes shone with irony. 'Among us here there are nine that came for the same reason I did. They know about fighting. Mr Carlyle that don't worry me. If there is a fight some of them could get hurt. They got friends among the ranchers. You understand?'

Tug nodded and the large man spoke again. 'We have a law-book man with us. He says if they come onto our land and start a fight we have the right to defend ourselves, but that's not what we want.'

Tug nodded again. 'You got an idea?'

'Talk, Mr Carlyle. I can tell what I saw when that storeman was shot in the back. I don't know the law. I know what I saw.' The large settler locked both work-hardened hands atop the table looking steadily at Tug. 'I want to catch them before there is a fight. I want to do it tonight when they are camped.'

Tug was beginning to understand. For the third time he inclined his head. He knew something about stealth. 'You want to brace them before they're ready come morning?'

'Yes.'

Tug scratched where one of Mary Todd's fleas had bitten him. 'Do you know where they are?'

'Yes. Maybe four, five miles from here.'

Tug stood up. 'It's got to be done soon.'

'Will you ride with us?'

Tug smiled. 'Any time you're ready.'

The large man arose and pushed out a big hand. As they shook he said, 'We should start now.'

That made sense. Dawn was some hours away but there was a fair distance to be covered. Tug and Freiberg went outside into a still warm night where a new moon shone.

Southward there was the sound of activity. Freiberg led the way. Where starlight shone, men appeared as dark wraiths. There was very little conversation. An older man approached Freiberg. They spoke briefly in a language Tug did not understand before the older man rejoined his companions.

Other men appeared leading horses. Tug watched them join the main group and was impressed. He'd had no idea how many people lived in the settlement until this moment and while he made no attempt to count them, by rough estimate he guessed there were no less than twenty, perhaps a tad more, and they were armed with rifles, a few carbines and every man wore a shellbelt and a holstered sidearm.

Walt appeared tense and unsmiling. He brushed Tug's arm. 'I rigged out your tall horse. He's at the corral with my outfit. Tug, they wanted you along.'

Someone led up a 1,200-pound sorrel horse and handed the reins to Freiberg. He tested the cinch, patted the large animal and faced Walt. 'Are you ready?'

Walt was, he took Tug with him to the corral where their animals were tied outside, unlooped his reins and said, 'You know the plan?'

Tug nodded. 'That many riders, Walt, aren't goin' to sneak up on a deaf man.'

Walt swung astride. As he was adjusting his booted carbine he said, 'We'll try.'

Tug mounted his thoroughbred, shoved the saddle boot under the fender and followed Skinner.

Freiberg and another settler had rifles balanced across the swells of their saddles.

When everyone was a-horseback the two leaders led out.

A dog barked; a few houses showed lights; not a word passed among the riders. Tug looked back and around. It was difficult to read faces in poor light. He had to assume the settlers were solid in their purpose, but as a war party they left something to be desired, in appearance anyway.

A younger man came out of the trees as the crowd began the climb to overhead forested country. He took the lead.

Part way along, another apparition appeared to join the scout in the lead.

Tug's spirits began to rise. His companions might look like a band of farmers on horseback but evidently someone had shaped them up.

A wiry, short man eased up beside Tug and nodded without smiling. He rode in silence for a fair distance before saying, 'It better work.'

Tug agreed but not so loud.

There was a hint of a chill in the late

night which was one thing riding through a forest did not mitigate.

The thin man offered Tug a well-gnawed plug. Tug shook his head. He had never mastered the art of chewing tobacco.

Walt appeared on Tug's right side and leaned to speak. 'We got the fee lawyer along.' Walt paused. 'He was sober.'

That statement established the wispy man's settlement credentials for Tug Carlyle.

The pair of scouting guides held to a fairly straight course. They had been scouting up the posse riders from Bridgeport since about sunset.

Tug guessed about how far they had come when one of the scouts held up his arm and halted. In the forward distance a horse nickered. The other scout went ahead leaving the halted homesteaders in almost total darkness among huge old tall trees where nothing grew but trees.

There was a palaver up where Carl

Freiberg and several others held a council. It was clear that they were close to their objective.

Someone levered a rifle and was instantly sworn at in hushed indignation. Tug revised his estimate of their position upwards. They were very close to the posse camp.

Freiberg swung to the ground to go among the mounted men. He detailed homesteaders to go from here on foot and without noise as they made a large surround. Tug heard him say, 'A rifle butt don't make noise,' as he divided the party. Three men were to be horse-holders. Everyone else was to join in making a silent surround, no one was to fire a weapon.

When Freiberg reached Tug he said, 'You come with me.'

Tug dismounted, lifted out his saddle gun and followed the big man.

Either the same horse or another one trumpeted in the night some distance ahead. Tug expected someone up there to be interested. Horses didn't just arbitrarily trumpet at night.

It happened but not until one of the horses being left behind with the horse-holders decided to answer. His whinny was pitched high and loud.

Up ahead through the forest giants a man called in a rough voice, 'They're tryin' to steal our horses!'

There was nothing wrong with the idea as a tactic but clearly setting the posse riders afoot was not Freiberg's plan.

The large older man looked around for Tug, leaned and said, 'When Walt whistles, come with me to their camp. Don't draw your gun.'

It was a long wait. To make a surround without alerting the men from Bridgeport what was happening required time.

As they waited Freiberg spoke in a low rumble. 'There are thirteen of them. They have a man with their horses. Walt is to take care of him first then whistle that they are surrounded.'

Tug was impressed. The big

sauerkraut-eater must have been quite a soldier where he came from.

One of the scouts who had led them came around a huge tree to tell Freiberg there were two guards with the horses. He was still explaining this when the shrill, loud whistle sounded.

Freiberg visibly tensed inside his heavy riding coat, jerked his head and started walking. Tug followed, Winchester nestled in the crook of his arm.

Someone up ahead let out a high-pitched squawk. A man with a deep rough voice said, 'Who are you? What'n hell do you think you're doing?'

He got a curt reply. 'Taking your gun. Stand up and shut up!'

The camp had been made in one of those rare small clearings. Puny night light showed it adequately to men whose eyes had been accustomed to forest darkness.

Someone up there cursed and another posseman was more sanguine. 'I told you they'd do somethin' like this.

Remember what you said? In'ians do this, civilized folks don't.'

The surround was complete and its men began a slow advance to tighten it. Roused posse riders came awake rubbing their eyes. One man reached for his Winchester and was struck senseless from behind.

The unmistakable but unpleasant voice of the Brighton constable was raised.

'Who the hell are you?' That was followed by the sound of a falling man.

The unmistakable accented growl of Carl Freiberg broke the stillness. 'Don't touch that gun!'

The surprise was complete. Possemen who had been in the saddle most of the day and had been sleeping like logs gradually stirred.

Freiberg gave another order. 'No guns. Throw them away. Sit up. Where is Felton and the other constable?'

The 'other constable' was unconscious at the feet of a moccasin-shod homesteader who leaned, yanked

Kellogg until the Brighton lawman came groggily to his senses. The homesteader hoisted him to his feet and steadied him.

Kellogg turned slowly. He was obviously in pain. He and his companions were completely surrounded and outnumbered. Kellogg looked for something to sit on, found someone's upended saddle and sat down. If he'd been hit hard there would have been blood. There was no broken hide but a lump was forming.

Kellogg leaned with his head in his hand, saw Felton and said, 'Dumb clod-hoppin' sons of bitches are they?'

Ames Felton was motionless and soundless. The years of harassing homesteaders without resistance had made him bold. Even in poor light he could recognize faces of men he'd troubled.

It required time to gather the guns and make sure they had them all. This was accomplished with a few growls but no conversation.

Carl Freiberg had their prisoners bunched around their horse equipment. There were eleven of them, all locals except for the men from Brighton and one of them started his day early by getting a cud tucked into his cheek after which he expectorated once and looked up at the armed riflemen behind him as he said, 'You boys tore it this time. Buckin' the law'll bring in more lawmen than you can count.'

This man spoke without fear. His companions were both mute and fearful. With the guns gathered, several settlers went horse hunting. When they found the posse horses they stripped them, got them headed back the way they had come and choused them.

That fearless posseman groaned then swore with feeling. It would be one hell of a long hike back in rough country and he had a bad ankle.

Felton watched Frank Kellogg; he had willingly conceded leadership of the Bridgeport posse riders to the man from Brighton.

The squatters who had run off saddle stock returned with several saddle-bags whose contents they dumped in plain sight. There were tins of food, two derringers, a Bowie knife in a beaded sheath and boxes of long-barrelled and short-barrelled ammunition.

Frank Kellogg moved to arise. The man behind him lent a hand which Kellogg jerked free of as he glared defiance. He snarled at one of his Brighton riders. 'Stupid dirt farmers! Cal, when we get back I'm goin' to kick your butt up between your shoulders.'

The man he had addressed would not meet the Brighton lawman's glare, but when he looked elsewhere several homesteaders, including Carl Freiberg, were looking at him.

Walt Skinner moved toward the seated posseman and spoke to the big farmer behind him without looking away from the man Kellogg had threatened.

'Is this him, Carl?'

Freiberg moved closer. It was dark,

with limited visibility. He had to lean before he said, 'That's him!'

This small drama held the others silent until the man sitting in front of Freiberg said, 'I know you. I've seen you'n your wagon down in Brighton.'

Freiberg straighted up. 'When was the last time you saw me?'

'The day that feller yonder robbed the bank'n the store. You was down near the smithy.'

The larger man nodded. 'I saw you too. I saw you shoot that storekeeper in the back.'

For seconds there was silence, then the seated man twisted to stand up and said, 'You damned liar! I shot at the feller yonder when he busted out of town in a dead run.'

Frank Kellogg was looking steadily at the upset posseman. Without looking away from him he said, 'Squatter . . . '

Carl faced the Brighton lawman. 'I was southward near the smithy when the shooting began. I turned to watch the outlaw run for it on a leggy big horse. I saw this man come out of a dog trot, aim and fire at the storekeeper. He hit him squarely in the back. That's the gospel truth. You can believe it or not but it's the truth. He was maybe sixty, eighty feet from where the storeman was standing out front of his store with a rifle. He raised his hand and shot the storekeeper. It wasn't no accident. The outlaw was riding hard bent double. He was to the far left. This man didn't turn to shoot at him. He shot the storekeeper in front of him and up the road maybe a hundred feet. Deliberately shot him.'

13

A Workable Proposition

An increasing chill came in among the trees to the small place where the homesteaders and their captives were bunched up.

A squatty, burly man buttoned into a heavy coat whose empty holster was on the outside addressed Frank Kellogg. 'I told you, Frank, the bullet come from behind not in front. Now are you satisfied?'

For the constable from Brighton it had always been hard to admit being wrong. He put a sulphurous stare on the burly, short man without speaking. Not until one of the homesteaders said, 'Hang the son of a bitch. There's plenty of trees.'

That stirred Kellogg. 'You don't hang anyone.'

Ames Felton said nothing. In fact, he seemed willing to be left out of all discussions.

Carl Freiberg said, 'It's closer to our settlement than it is to Bridgeport. We go there. Get up. *Get up!*'

The distance was indeed shorter but it was still a fair distance in country not created for walking, except maybe for Indians and there hadn't been any Indians in the Spanish Bit country in ten years.

The lawman from Brighton had the grandaddy of all headaches. Not until they broke clear of forested uplands was the lump noticeable. Streaks of daylight showed up high; down close, the world remained gloomily dark.

Frank Kellogg abruptly sank down on a punky deadfall. He could walk no further.

A homesteader astride one of those 1,400-pound pudding-footed horses took him up behind the cantle and the hike was continued.

Along about the time they were amid

the last tier of trees before starting downslope it was possible to see lights. Nearly every house had some kind of illumination.

Farmers were naturally early risers but not this early, and breaking clear of forested country, starting down the stumped-over downslope the chill noticeably increased; dawn was not far off.

Frank Kellogg's recovery was slow. Whoever had hit him over the head with a rifle barrel must have leaned into his work. There was still no blood but the bump was by this time the size of a pullet egg and Kellogg did not have to act the part of a man in pain, he was in pain.

There was an old man, hatless and leaning on an ancient rifle who met the riders at Freiberg's corral. He counted the riders, came up with too many and started over. A woman wrapped in a long army coat also counted. When she pronounced a number the old gummer scowled but offered no alternative,

241

mainly because he wasn't quite illiterate but was close enough to have made a habit of accepting other people's ciphering for many years.

The old man squinted as the horsemen were dismounting. Maybe he couldn't do numbers but his eyesight was excellent. He said, 'Hell, that's Frank Kellogg from down Brighton way. Carl? Hey, Carl?'

Neither Freiberg or the others heeded the old man. They were fully occupied, several left for home, others hobbled their animals outside the corral for whatever reason and others turned their mounts in.

Freiberg herded the captives toward his barn, left them there under guard and went to the house where an anxious pair of women were waiting.

He returned with a hissing lantern, told the possemen to sit on the ground and, starting with the weasel-faced man named Cal Mitchell, read the riot act, including the statement that Brighton lawmen had no authority in the Spanish

Bit country, also known as the Meadow Homestead settlement.

He repeated what he'd said before about witnessing the outright murder down at Brighton.

When he was finished, he looked at Walt and Tug but neither of them spoke so Freiberg addressed Constable Kellogg.

'If you got your money back, then what?'

Kellogg's headache was diminishing in a centralized way. He said, 'Got to be more'n your word Cal Mitchell shot the storekeeper; all the same I'll lock him up when we get back to Brighton an' see if anyone else seen what you said you saw. I can tell you one thing: Mr Forsythe, the storekeeper, an' Cal wasn't on speakin' terms. He told me that; the reason he said was that Cal owed a bill at the store for a year an' made no effort to pay up.'

Walt and Tug leaned against a saddle pole, spectators and silent. Carl Freiberg faced Mitchell, a scrawny individual with a slit for a mouth and eyes that darted. Mitchell spoke before Freiberg could.

'I told him two times I'd pay up. He was disagreeable about it. Said he'd haul me before the journeyman judge next time he come to town. I shot high. That feller on the leggy horse was gettin' away. I tried to drop a ball on him.'

'How high?' Tug dryly said.

'Maybe eight, ten feet high and the storekeeper ain't that tall.'

Kellogg interrupted. 'This isn't no court, Freiberg. You figure to keep us prisoners here, because if you do the law'll make charges against you of — '

Freiberg's growl interrupted. 'You're not prisoners. But sneaking up on us in the dark . . . we got a right to defend ourselves. You can go any time you want to. Mister, don't come back. Next time we'll hang the lot of you. Start walking. Leave the guns here. Constable, when you get back to Brighton, I give you my word, I saw him shoot that man in the back. Deliberate.' Freiberg went to lean on the edge of a manger, waiting. The possemen acted wary. Freiberg shook his head. 'We don't shoot people in the back.'

Walt spoke for the first time. 'Mister Kellogg, the money'll be short. Constable Felton helped himself.'

Kellogg jerked his head for the Bridgeport lawman to walk up front with him and led off out of the barn. He abruptly halted and turned back.

'Where's the money from the bank'n the store?'

Walt looked steadily at Tug who didn't move. He was leaning with crossed arms. Walt continued to look. Tug shook his head, said something under his breath, went after the saddle-bags, took them to Kellogg and shoved them so hard Kellogg staggered.

Not a word was exchanged.

Dawn was breaking, the chill had been steadily increasing since shy of midnight.

It would be a long walk. The

homesteaders dispersed. It was getting close to chore time. Carl Freiberg, Walt and Tug lingered at the barn until the bear-like older man said, 'There'll be breakfast,' and waited for the younger men to respond.

Walt spoke to Tug. 'If you'd like to stay there's a good piece of land over here. It's the original Spanish Bit claim.'

Tug nodded without speaking, left the barn, got his horse and rode up the slope heading east. In the timber he cut the sign of walking men, made a wide sashay around it and rode steadily until he came to the stumped-over country and could see Bridgeport.

Activity was minimal as he angled down toward the village. He entered from the south-west, left his horse at the café tie rack and went to the jailhouse, searched until he found the keys and went to the cell where Beth said, 'I wondered whether it would be you or Ames.'

As he unlocked and opened the door,

he said, 'Ames'll be along later. He's walkin' with the others. We got time for breakfast if you're of a mind.'

As they left the jailhouse, several villagers saw them cross to the café. It wouldn't be long before word got around.

Tug sat at the counter as Beth went to work in her kitchen. She called questions which he answered cryptically. Losing the money didn't just kill his notion of settling, it also left him almost broke.

When she put a platter of fried spuds and eggs in front of him she asked, 'Let me guess. The settlers outnumbered them.'

He considered the food. 'Somethin' like that. Beth, I gave back the money.'

She smiled without speaking. The look on his face was readable. 'Tug?'

'What?'

'It don't matter . . . are you ready to settle down?'

He nodded. 'But I figured to use that money as a stake.'

She let the smile fade. 'I bought some land over at the squatter settlement. Forty acres. I want to settle over there.'

He reached for the coffee cup. 'They . . . I never farmed in my life.' He half emptied the cup and put it aside. 'I like it over there.'

'So do I. That's why I bought the land. It adjoins some land with an old adobe house on it. Years back they found an old Spanish spade bit in the house. They called their settlement the Spanish Bit country but later called it The Meadow, or Meadowland. Tug?'

The eggs were getting cold. He looked at them. She said, 'You want to try it? If it don't work out you can ride on.'

He looked up at her. 'You mean the both of us?'

She rolled her eyes. 'Somethin' like that.'

'Marry up?'

She reached for the coffee cup. 'I'll warm it up.'

'Wait a minute.'

She put the cup down. *Men! Strong as oak and twice as thick.*

'Beth.'

'Maybe you'd do better just to ride on, Tug.'

'No. It's just that . . . are you sure you want to do this?'

'I'm sure.'

He repeated something he'd said earlier. 'I'm no farmer.'

'No one's born a farmer, Tug. That food's gettin' cold.'

'Beth, I've never even kissed you.'

She leaned far over, closed her eyes and puckered up. He also leaned. After the kiss she said, 'If you don't own a razor I've got one.'

He lifted out her pistol and placed it on the counter. She ignored the gun. 'Eat your breakfast.'

As he began eating, she leaned with one hand beneath her chin, looking at him. 'You want to know somethin', Tug? I been wonderin' for years whatever became of you.'